PRINT THE LEGEND

The Previously Unpublished Memoir
of Alison Stanton Bradshaw

"A vivid, fast-paced adventure set against the backdrop of the wild high country of northern New Mexico. In great western fashion, the characters are earnest and honest, but ruthless and deadly when hard pressed."

Stephen Zimmer
Author of *People of the Cimarron Country*

"Warren Smith's *Print the Legend* evokes the mystical attraction that beckoned good and bad sojourners to linger awhile in New Mexico's Sangre de Cristo Mountains. Smith's characters are full of contradictions and longing for redemption—even as fortunes are won and lost."

Michael Martin Murphey
Singer, songwriter, and Western historian

"Westerns became favorite Hollywood fare in the first half of the 20th century. In the second half many added a touch of melancholy about the frontier's closing, along with a tragic sensibility of man's limits and the omnipresence of death. For the 21st century Warren Smith melds action, tragedy, and beauty in a novel that sweeps readers through a New Mexico landscape soon littered with corpses."

Marvin Olasky
Editor in chief, *WORLD Magazine*

PRINT THE LEGEND

The Previously Unpublished Memoir of Alison Stanton Bradshaw

A Novel by

WARREN COLE SMITH

This book is dedicated to Missy, my Ali.

Cover artwork: "The Creak of Leather"
  Courtesy of Jeff Segler. Used by Permission.

Library of Congress Control Number: 2017942302
ISBN: 978-0-9974267-3-1

 Published by Eagle Trail Press www.EagleTrailPress.com info@EagleTrailPress.com

"This is the West, sir.
When the legend becomes fact,
print the legend."

— from *The Man Who Shot Liberty Valance*

"For West is where we all plan to go some day. It is where you
go when the land gives out and the old-field pines encroach.
It is where you go when you get the letter saying: Flee, all is
discovered. It is where you go when you look down at the blade
in your hand and the blood on it. It is where you go when you
are told that you are a bubble on the tide of empire. It is where
you go when you hear that 'thar's gold in them-thar hills.' It is
where you go to grow up with the country. It is where you go
to spend your old age. Or it is just where you go."

— Robert Penn Warren

PROLOGUE

My name is Alison Stanton Bradshaw. I live in Los Angeles, and the year is 1940. They say we are about to go to war with countries half-a-world away.

I know little about such things because, you see, I am an old woman now. It's not that I don't understand what is going on. I am not senile. I read the papers. I listen to the radio. And on Wednesdays I dress up and call for my car and sit quietly on leather seats as we roll out of Beverly Hills south toward downtown. We arrive at the California Club, the club my husband helped to build, in the city my husband helped to build. The bellman opens the door to my car and offers me his gloved hand, which I take. He helps me out of the car. If people are around— and they usually are—they stop and wait for me to pass. They whisper to one another. I am too old to hear what they whisper, but before I lost my hearing I heard them, and they are saying the same things now.

They say, "She is the last of a breed."

They say, "She made her money in the movies" or "Her husband made millions in real estate" or "I hear she's still the richest woman in California." Once I even heard someone say, "Before he found God, he was an outlaw and a killer."

No, I cannot hear them, but I know what they are saying, and it is all—after a fashion—true.

I take the elevator up one level and walk slowly into the women's dining room of the California Club. (I smile as I write this: these days, slowly is the only way I can walk.) I will sit for two hours, and I will talk some, but mostly I listen, for my hearing is not that far gone. I listen to these women who are married to the most powerful men in California, which today makes them among the most powerful men in the nation.

So I know what is going on around me.

I also know what has gone by. I know I was married to a great man, greater than the husbands of any of these women, though in the early days you might not have known it. I see the young women – the daughters and the granddaughters. They are in the full flower of their beauty, and I now see in their eyes their disdain toward me. They see me as old and bent over. They do not understand that they, too, will one day be as old and stooped as I am. Neither do they understand that while they disdain me, I pity them. They have their looks, it's true. But their looks will fade and they will still be as foolish as they are today. In a way, they are right to see me as something altogether different, altogether other.

If only they knew. Just how different. Just how…other.

In one sense I am not so different from the women of the California Club. In my day they called me a great beauty, too. That, of course, is not for a lady to say about herself. Still, it was true, and so I say it. The truth has always mattered to me, and I have always been a woman who knew her own mind. I have trusted my own judgment. Though to speak my mind out loud….That is not something I have always done.

But, as I said, I am an old woman now. No one is left alive to protect, so I will say what is on my mind in the pages that follow, and you can draw your own conclusions about whether I am still a lady, or—for that matter—ever was.

What I do not want to leave to your own conclusion is this: we saw—and did—some remarkable things. When my husband died, not so many years ago when reckoned in the grand sweep of time, the newspapermen swarmed around and told a few of the stories. More recently, the college professors have come calling. They scoff at the newspapermen and their tall tales and say I must let them tell the true history. But the newspapermen and the college professors went away, and they wrote what they wrote. And most of it is, in its way, true.

It is just not the whole truth. That is why I am telling my story to you, my children, and anyone else you choose to share this story with. This is a story you will not read in the newspapers or the history books. You will finally know what happened in the high country of northern New Mexico a lifetime ago.

This story is my confession.

To Colorado City
and Denver

Colorado
New Mexico

Raton Pass

Valle Vidal

Santa Fe Trail
Mountain Branch

Raton

Moreno
Valley

Cimarron

Springer

Taos

Wildhorse
Park

Rayado

Rio Grande River

Wagon
Mound

Pecos
Mountains

Santa Fe

Las
Vegas

Lamy
Station

To El Paso and Old Mexico

Map created from the hand-drawn original by Dave Stanton

Chapter 1

Raton, New Mexico, 1881

The Old Santa Fe Trail left Colorado by climbing over Raton Pass and dropping into the town of Raton. Then it headed southwest—along the edge of the mountains some people now call Vermejo Park—toward Cimarron.

On this July night, the moon was a few days past full, which meant it brightened the sky for most of the early evening as two horsemen rode south over Raton Pass and, after two hours at a steady clip, came to the edge of town.

The moon was now down. The night was still. Only the crickets made their small music, and down by the livery stable a horse stamped restlessly, lifting his head, ears pricked, as the two riders glided quietly by.

A third rider, a big man who sat easy in the saddle, rode down from out of the mountains that bordered Raton to the west. He came down a draw and walked his horse along the alleyway leading to Raton's main street. This third rider did not emerge upon the street, but drew rein in the deepest shadows beside the general store. He bowed his head as if to nap, and he closed his eyes, but he was far from sleep. He was concentrating, listening for the approach of the two riders he knew would be coming down the street.

So far these three riders saw no sign of Brad Bradshaw, the fourth man and the leader of this small gang. But the big man—

everyone called him Hondo—just smiled. He would have been disappointed to see Brad one second earlier than necessary. That was what made Brad such a genius at bank robbing. He planned everything out to the second. No surprises, no wasted motion, and no unnecessary risks.

Brad would be exactly where he needed to be exactly when he needed, and the other men knew it.

The two riders coming down from Raton Pass went by, turning at the last minute in a perfect column right to stop before the bank. The two men dismounted, and each held a rifle. With scarcely a sound, Hondo had fallen in behind them, but he did not stop in front of the bank. He guided his horse into another alleyway along the side of the bank building, where the shadows were so deep that he was hard to see.

As he dismounted he was careful to hold upright a fruit jar. It was a small jar, but Hondo treated it with respect.

It was just then that Bradshaw appeared. He opened a side door of the bank building—from the inside. Hondo smiled to himself. Brad was already inside. Of course he was. Where else would he be?

"It's an old box," Brad said as Hondo stepped inside with the fruit jar and its delicate contents. "Nothing to worry about."

Hondo smiled, because he knew Brad was always worrying. That's also one of the qualities that made him great at this work. Still, Hondo was reassured by Brad's presence and his words. Hondo's eyes had adjusted in the alleyway, and he moved quickly past Brad in the darkness. He squatted before the big iron safe.

Brad walked back to the door for one last look down the empty street. It was not too late to call the whole thing off, and Bradshaw—as their leader—was the man to make that call, if in fact the call needed to be made. It would not be the first time.

That had happened a year earlier, in Old Colorado City—what they now call Colorado Springs—a hundred miles to the north. They had planned the job all summer, aiming to hit the bank in September and hauling off with enough money to allow them to make it through the winter in some sort of comfort. But that afternoon a freak fall snowstorm started. By midnight, when they had planned to make their move, a foot of snow covered the ground. Bradshaw knew that most of it would be gone the next day, but on this night it would have made their escape into the mountains all but impossible.

So he told the boys to stand down. They were disappointed, but they trusted Bradshaw. The next night the job went off without a hitch. They rode two days west into the mountains. Bradshaw split up the money, and then he split up the gang for the winter, telling them not to draw attention to themselves.

Now they were back together, and Brad would not call off tonight's work. He looked up and down the street through the front window of the bank. Brad Bradshaw saw no one except his own men.

Hondo sat cross-legged on the floor in front of the safe, practicing his craft. Through the window, standing in the shadows next to the bank was Romney, a lapsed Mormon who was making up for lost time with women, liquor, caffeine, and tobacco. Romney stood in the shadows, almost out of sight until he lit a cigarette. The flash of the match showed an angry, angular face. He was the old man of this gang, though—truth be told—none of them had yet turned thirty, though Romney and Bradshaw were close.

The fourth and final man in this small gang was a Cherokee Indian named Jeffcoat. We never knew his first name. He was short and thick, but not fat—pure bone and muscle. Jeffcoat's grandfather had been an important man, a chief, with the Cherokees in Georgia. He was an educated man. But the Trail of Tears broke him. He died somewhere near Memphis in the 1830s as his people were herded west. The great chief's son, Jeffcoat's father, had walked the rest of the way to Oklahoma without his father, grieving his father, vowing to avenge the death of his father.

So he grew up to hate the white man, but also—in that strange logic of the human heart—also to hate his own father, who had allowed the white man to defeat him. The only problem was that Jeffcoat's father could not take his hate out on his own

3

dead father, so he took it out on his son. He beat Jeffcoat as a boy. Eventually the boy fled home and took out his own anger and pain on the world.

That is, until he met Brad. Brad had taken him in and treated him like a brother. No, not a brother, exactly, but like a man. Brad picked Jeffcoat up out of the gutter in Old Colorado City, sobered him up, and gave him work to do in the gang. What Jeffcoat felt for Brad was not love, exactly. Loyalty was perhaps a better word. But Jeffcoat would die for Brad, and Brad knew it.

Brad walked back to where Hondo was working on the safe. Though the night had turned cool, sweat beaded on the big man's face as he leaned into the steel drill bit. It bit into the softer iron of the safe. The first hole, at the top corner of the safe, was well started.

"You need a break?"

"No."

Hondo was, as I said, a craftsman, proud of his work. That's one of the reasons Brad wanted him in the gang. Hondo was also an orphan. We never knew just how his mother and father had died, only that Hondo had come from Louisiana. Along the way, he had gotten good with a rope, which is how he earned his nickname. A *hondo* is the eyelet at the end of a lariat, though as Hondo drifted west he learned the word also had another meaning: "deep." As in Arroyo Hondo, which means a "deep stream." Hondo came to love the double meaning of his name, and began to think of both his roping and his robbing as art.

Hondo made his way in the world using both gifts: roping strays and unbranded cattle. The strays he would return to their owners for the reward. The unbranded cattle he would sell.

It was all perfectly legal, even a service to the ranches. But with no family to keep him tied down, he drifted west into the Texas panhandle, where folks didn't know him. He had roped a small herd of branded and unbranded cows in the Palo Duro country and was planning to take them to Lubbock to sell. But there had been a lot of rustling in that part of the country, and before he had a chance to set out a group of hard men—hired guns—from the local "cattleman's association" came across Hondo's camp. They said they didn't believe Hondo hadn't rustled these cows, though the truth is they didn't want to believe. It was their job to find cattle rustlers, and Hondo fit the description close enough. They shipped him off to a Texas prison, where an old peterman showed him every way there was to crack a safe.

Hondo used to joke, "Before I went to prison, I was an honest man. I had to go to prison to learn how to be a crook."

He and Brad had gotten along from the beginning. They were both meticulous, even under pressure. Years later, Brad would say to me: "I was the director, but Hondo was the star."

Up the street somewhere a door slammed, and everyone froze. After a few seconds of quiet, a hand pump squeaked rhythmically. After a few seconds more, they could hear the water gushing into an empty tin bucket.

They waited in complete silence. Hondo stopped drilling, pulling the heavy drill out of the hole he was making in the safe, resting it in his lap. Another long minute passed before they finally heard a door close up the street, and then silence. Hondo replaced the drill in the hole and leaned into his job. Sweat trickled down his face, but he worked steadily, unhurried and confident.

Every second that passed increased the danger. Brad and his men knew these western towns only too well, and nobody got away with anything in any of them. They had all heard gangs brag about terrorizing towns, taking towns over, but that never happened. Every man in Raton had a rifle and knew how to use it. Every woman had a pistol, at least. Even the kids had guns, usually .22 single-shot rifles. "Pea-shooters," folks called them, but they could still kill a man if the bullet hit him in the right place. Brad had no illusions that he or any gang of outlaws could bully Raton or any other Western town.

Take the banker of this town, for example. He had been a colonel in the Union Army during the Civil War, and before that a young lieutenant in the War with Mexico. He had fought Indians and hunted buffalo. He might be a bank owner now, but

5

he had been a dangerous man once, and if the situation was right he could be—would be—a dangerous man again.

The saloonkeeper across the street from the bank—he'd been a guide and a buffalo hunter. The man who owned the general store had been the crack shot of his regiment during the Civil War, and after the war fought Indians in Wyoming and Nebraska. These were not soft city slickers, but men who had survived the wildness of the West, and were now imposing their will on that very wildness.

The whole town was like that. It was a time when every western town's population was made up of the daring, the adventurous, the skilled. Gunmen and outlaws were left alone so long as they kept to themselves in the lower-class saloons and contented themselves with the girls in the bawdy houses. But they were not to linger long, nor were they to look more than a glance at the wives and daughters of the town. That was something Brad Bradshaw learned the hard way.

An insect droned by in the darkness, and somewhere a mourning dove called. Brad leaned against the door jamb and waited, listening to the sound of the drill.

There came a moment in every job, Brad told me later, when he felt a sudden hot rush of anger and despair. It was that moment when it was too late to back out, but too early to celebrate. That moment when he vowed this would be the last job. That moment when he knew he was risking his life for a few dollars, and he knew it was a foolish and damnable proposition.

That moment when he wished he could turn back the clock to the last moment before he became an outlaw. No, that would not be early enough... to the last moments before the war, that war in which a part of him—and a lot of other men—had died, or gotten lost, or at least misplaced for a long, long time.

But would backing up the clock even to the war be back far enough? Who can say what chain of events brought any of us to where we are now? Would breaking just one of the many links in that chain change the course of a man's life? Does fate, or destiny, or God, or whatever it is that pushes us inexorably into the current of time ever really let us swim back to the bank and get out? We can paddle back and forth, from shore to shore, maybe, but does the river not roll on down to the sea?

Brad didn't know—at least not then—but he would say later that joining the army was the beginning. He was a big, strapping Tennessee boy, but everyone in the area knew he was just a boy. So for years, through 1861, '62, and '63, he watched others go off to war. Some of them came home with stories of great heroism, and some of them—of course—did not come home at all.

Finally, he had had enough of hearing other people's stories, and he wanted to make stories of his own. One night he saddled his horse and rode east. All through the night he rode, and all the next day. Then another day, and another. Non-stop. He had left Tennessee and entered northern Mississippi, then into Alabama. He was muddy and hollow-eyed and looked ten years older than the 15-year-old boy he really was. He had no trouble finding an outfit that would sign him on. It was now 1864 and the Confederacy was beginning to lose badly. Any man—or boy—who could shoot a rifle was welcome by then. So Brad Bradshaw saw war, and heroism, and he saw a lot of men die.

And, of course, he gathered stories of his own, but they were stories so horrible he would never tell them, some of them not even to me. I think it was the war that turned him into an outlaw. He had seen men who were supposed to be on the right side of the law, on "God's side" in the war, do things so horrible he couldn't talk about them. Men for whom killing had become nearly as natural as breathing. If this is what it meant to be on the right side of the law, well…. Many years later I asked Brad if he ever stopped believing in God. He thought about that question for a bit and said, "No. No, I never stopped believing in God. But I went through a stretch where I thought he was a real son-of-a-bitch."

But on this night, Brad was not thinking about such questions in quite these ways. He was just wondering why and how he had become such a damned fool. He had a good plan, and a good team. He had thought about everything there was to think about. Still, he could not shake the notion that he was a fool. Any man who tried to rob a bank was. Years later he would say, "When you go to rob a bank, there's a million things you need to think of, and if you miss one of them, you can end up at the end of a rope. Not only that, if you can think of half of them, you're a genius. And if you were a genius you wouldn't be robbing banks in the first place."

II

Hondo rested, mopping sweat from his forehead. The first hole was finished. Brad picked up a bar of home-made soap and began stopping up the crack around the door of the safe. Out in the street, one of the horses stamped and Hondo placed his drill in the new position and went to work. The iron showed white under the bite of the steel bit.

The dove called again, a lonesome call, inquiring and plaintive. But Brad was glad to hear it, since it likely meant no one was out and about.

He slapped a mosquito on his neck.

The time passed, and that increased the tension among the gang. Romney no longer leaned against the building. His nonchalance was gone. He was sweating, too. Only Jeffcoat, ever stoic, seemed unperturbed.

Romney hissed suddenly and Brad touched Hondo on the shoulder. The drill ceased to move. In the silence Brad could hear the slow ticking of the bank clock.

On the cross street a few doors away they could hear two horses walking, two sleepy riders on sleepy horses. They crossed Main Street and vanished in the darkness, with the muzzles of two rifles on them all the way. When they had been gone a full minute, Bradshaw spoke to Hondo and the big man returned to work. He had not so much as turned his head to look.

Brad grew impatient. His mouth was dry and he was getting jittery. No, not getting jittery. Rather, he was letting show the jitteriness he now felt all the time. Brad had learned that when a man took the wrong side of the law, every man was his enemy.

You became fair game for any chance passer-by who felt like taking a shot at you. You became an enemy of the people. What was worse, the people became your enemy.

In the street a horse stamped again impatiently. Romney lit another cigarette. Hondo was through with his drilling, and he finished soaping the crack around the door. Then he made a cup of soap around the lock. To this he attached a short fuse.

Bradshaw stepped out back and picked up an old mattress he had taken from the town dump on the edge of town. He brought it through the back door, and placed it against the safe. He wrapped the safe carefully in ragged blankets from the stable out back, and then he and Hondo quietly and carefully opened all the bank windows so the concussion would not break the glass. The fall of broken glass had been known to awaken people when the concussion itself had not.

Brad went to the door. He glanced from Jeffcoat to Romney. "Ready?"

Each gave him a thumbs up. Jeffcoat stepped out to stand with the horses, holding the reins of them all.

Brad glanced over his shoulder and whispered, "All right, Hondo."

Outside, the watching men lifted their rifles, and Jeffcoat murmured something to the horses. Hondo had lighted a cigarette, and now he touched it to the fuse. It hissed sharply and both men inside ducked out of the door and crouched close against the wall, waiting.

The mourning dove called, but its cry disappeared in the muffled boom from within the bank.

Hondo and Brad rushed the safe. The acrid smell bit at their nostrils. The door, blasted open, was hanging by one hinge.

Brad raked the contents off the lip of the safe and into a feed sack Hondo held open for him. He had more than one sack, but they did not need it. This safe was nearly empty. No stacks of gold. A small package of bills and a tray of coins—though, to be sure, some of the coins were in fact gold. Still, it was a disappointing sight, a few hundred dollars at most. After cleaning out the safe, Brad ransacked a drawer and found a small package of bills—only a few dollars more.

Somewhere down the street a door slammed, and instantly Romney fired. The report racketed against the false-fronted stores, slapping back and forth across the narrow street.

The four men heard a shout, then the heavy bellow of a buffalo gun. Jeffcoat replied with a shot from his Winchester.

Bradshaw straightened to his feet.

"Let's get out of here."

Hondo crossed the floor in three great strides and ducked swiftly around the corner to his horse. Brad went out the back door, almost tripping over the crowbar he had used to force open the door when they entered. From the street came a steady sound of gunshots.

Romney was already in the saddle when Bradshaw rounded the building, and Jeffcoat had his bridle looped over his arm and was firing methodically up the street.

"All right," said Bradshaw.

The Indian slid up into his saddle in a fluid motion, not using the stirrup until he was astride the horse. The four riders wheeled into the deeper shadows of an alley. A window went up and a rifle barrel was thrust out at them, but Hondo put a .44 bullet through the glass above the rifleman's head. With the shattering of the glass came a startled yelp and the rifle fell to the ground outside.

The four riders scattered through a mass of scrub oak that gave way to ponderosa pine trees. They splashed across a stream, and turned south, quickly putting the town behind them. They did not ride fast, holding their horses for the necessary drive of speed should pursuit be organized in time to worry them.

Behind them in the town a few wild shots sounded, but after crossing the stream they had taken themselves out of sight and out of range.

Brad held the men at a steady pace for about two miles. Then he turned at right angles and rode into the stream, with the others following. They crossed it to a ledge of rock, then turned back into the stream and rode downstream for a quarter of a mile. They came out on the far side and onto a sandy draw left bare and dry by a wide turn in the stream.

Tracks left in that deep sand were only dimples, shapeless and impossible to identify, or even to estimate as to the time they were made.

"How'd we do?"

Romney was eager, easily the most hot-headed of the group. He still believed that every score was going to be a big one. He had yet to learn that even the most carefully planned robberies might net exactly nothing—unless one counted the bullets fired.

"The gold was gone. All of it. There's maybe a couple of hundred in change and small bills."

"Hell."

The opinion was scarcely open to debate, and nobody felt like talking. Even an empty bank does not like to have its safe blown up, and the citizenry would like the sport of the chase. Western towns—and Brad knew it all too well—had little excitement, so a bank robbery gives everybody a chance to have a fast ride and do a little shooting. They were forming a posse even now, and every man would be a tough, trail-seasoned veteran.

Brad led the way up the canyon as if it were broad daylight. He knew this country. Years earlier Colfax County had been his home. Even in the darkness he knew where he was, and when he felt the sudden coolness in the air he knew they were at a cut in the mesa wall, and he turned sharply to the right. When he saw the notch in the skyline above them, he started his horse up the steep slide of talus.

It was a hard scramble for the horses, but it left no tracks, and at the top of the mesa they drew up to let the horses catch their wind. Pursuit would be impossible until daylight, a good three hours off.

They were now in the high, wild country west of Raton— Vermejo Park, Ponil country, and the Valle Vidal. They would find no towns for 50 miles in that direction. It was ridge and canyon country. Fairly easy going if you stayed in the canyons, but that was not the straightest line to where they were headed—a pole corral high on the shoulder of Little Costilla Peak. A day before, they had pieced the corral together themselves using all the aspen deadfall they could find, not wanting to take the time to cut down more trees than they had to. That was where they kept their own four horses. By sunrise, they had made it. Nearby stood an old shack with its roof and one wall caved in.

Hondo made coffee and started breakfast. Jeffcoat stripped the saddles from the horses they had ridden and turned the animals lose with a slap on the rump. They had been borrowed without permission and would return to their home range. He saddled the horses waiting in the corral.

Over the small fire they smoked and drank their coffee. Nobody felt like talking. The job had started out with great promise, but it had failed. There was no other way to say it.

Nobody was hurt, nor had they hurt anybody. Had their escape been a few seconds slower or less carefully organized, one or more of them might be dead. Of this they had no doubt.

"Well," Romney said reluctantly, "even Jesse James pulled a couple of stick-ups that netted him nothing."

Nobody answered, so he added, "But they say he buried a million dollars in a cave in Missouri. I'd sure like to find that."

"Don't you believe it," Hondo said. "Anybody who wants to can get the figures. In sixteen years of outlawing the James gang took in less than four hundred thousand dollars. And they had to split that up six ways, sometimes more. They were down and out most of the time."

They finished their coffee in silence. Hondo dumped out the coffee grounds and kicked dirt over the fire. They took a last careful look around to make sure they hadn't forgotten anything, and then they mounted their own horses and rode out of the draw.

Brad was tired. His hard, wiry body relaxed to the easy movements of the horse. Brad often said that there's nothing better for the inside of a man than the outside of a horse. And most of the time that was true. The rhythm of riding a horse has calmed many a troubled mind. But on this day Brad's muscles ached with weariness and he desperately wanted to lie down somewhere under a tree and catch up on his sleep. But he could not, and that realization made anger and sadness well up in him. That was the worst part of this life. Somebody was always after you. The more successful you were as a bank robber, the more people were after you. There was no way to win, really. You just tried to keep from losing. To stay one step ahead. To hope—could he dare even to pray after some of the things he had done?—for a moment of peace.

It was now fully light. The sun came up and grew hot. Brad paused when they topped out on a ridge and surveyed the country before them, shimmering with heat waves.

Years later Brad would not talk about those days much, except when I pushed him. And even then he would act annoyed by my questions.

"Robbing banks is nothing but long rides without sleep, scarce food, and the fact that you're a preferred target for any man with a gun. There's nothing romantic about it."

III

They headed toward Cimarron, but they would not go there directly. They turned west into the vast wilderness of the Valle Vidal.

When Brad had been a young man, he had worked on all the ranches in the Cimarron country, but he had never felt at home on any of them. The Valle Vidal had been his sanctuary. Even in dry seasons you could find water. Elk and antelope roamed by the thousand. He worked mostly on the Chase Ranch, a 10,000-acre spread just north of Cimarron along the Ponil Creek and tucked in between the town and the hundreds of thousands of acres of the Valle.

It was mostly open range then, in the late 1860s, and mostly sheep country then. Colfax County didn't become cattle country until the late 1870s, when the railroads came through. But old Manley Chase ran some cattle into the high country, on the same shoulder of Little Costilla Peak that Brad knew would be the right spot to swap horses.

When the war ended, Brad knew he could not go home. It is hard to say exactly why he knew that, but he did. Years later he would say it was because he hated himself for some of the things he had done in the war, and he was afraid the people who knew him best would see how he had changed.

So he headed west, because in those days, that's where a young man headed who had no place else to go: West.

He had heard of Pike's Peak, and he wanted to see it. He figured he would ride across Texas and when he got to the mountains he would ride north until he came to it.

But riding across the Texas Panhandle and eastern New Mexico had nearly killed him. When he saw the Sangre de Cristo Mountains rising up in Colfax County, it looked like Heaven on Earth—Home.

Brad had no trouble signing on with Manley Chase, who sent him straightway into the Valle Vidal. Brad would be gone for months at a time, following the cattle from meadow to pasture, with just enough of an eye on them to keep the mountain lions away, exploring every canyon, every mesa, every stream and spring, every notch and draw.

Mr. Chase would send an old Mexican man in a wagon up Ponil Creek and into the Valle Vidal a couple of times a summer with sugar and salt and flour and coffee and whatever vegetables the gardens below were producing. The vegetables would be gone in a few days, but they broke the monotony of rabbit and deer. He didn't like to shoot elk. They were so large that he knew most of the meat would go to waste. Of course, the coffee was always welcome.

During those days, and even now, as his little gang rode west over the Vermejo country and into the Valle Vidal, Brad was never far from Cimarron—at least in his mind. The town was west and south from Raton, and due south of the Valle Vidal. The name of the town means "wild one," and in those days it certainly was that.

But Cimarron was also strangely civilized. It was hardscrabble country, to be sure, but the people it attracted were builders. Kit Carson had a home there before moving to Taos. Lucien Maxwell, of the massive million-acre Maxwell Land Grant, out of which Cimarron and all the area's ranches had been carved, had made his headquarters there.

Brad had been a puncher on those ranches, and he had once been foolish enough to think he might have found his home there. In those years just after the Civil War, the war that had scrambled everything for him, he thought he might be able to unscramble things here.

He had fallen in with another young man, Will Kane, and for a while they were closer than brothers. Years later, Brad finally got to the point where he could tell his war stories to me. But until then, he had told no one what he had been through. No one, that is, except Will, on those long days and nights in the Valle Vidal.

Will, like Brad, was a top hand, but he was a couple of years younger, and had missed the war altogether. Though Brad would often tell him how lucky he was that he had missed the war, Will always felt he had something to prove. I never heard of Will starting a fight, but he finished plenty of them.

In those days of open range it was possible to find half-wild unbranded stock high up in the backcountry, and occasionally when they wanted a night on the town they rounded up a few head of mavericks and drove them into Cimarron to sell. The trouble was that the big ranchers believed all stock, unbranded or not, belonged to them.

Will and Brad got along fine with old Manley Chase, who in the years right after the war was still mostly ranching sheep. If Will and Brad found a stray cow, old Mr. Chase didn't begrudge the boys from selling it off for a little extra spending money. But the other ranchers were not so forgiving, especially after the ranches in the Cimarron country turned to cattle in the 1870s. It was plain to see there were no brands on the yearlings Will and Brad found and sold by their own initiative up the canyons. But that didn't matter. They were warned off the range, effectively becoming outcasts in the Cimarron country.

During the winter that followed the two lived on strays and whatever work they could find, and it was the worst kind of work. The big ranches wouldn't hire them, but some of the smaller freeholders took pity on the young men and would let them hang around for a week or two and cut wood or break ice so the sheep could drink when it was 10 below. As they moved around the country, they continued to round up unbranded stock, only now they had grown less particular. If they happened to catch a few wearing brands…well, those big ranchers had robbed them of their livelihood and on some of the coldest night in the Cimarron country it took all their skill to keep their poor situation from robbing them of their lives.

Will and Brad were not bad men, but they had stopped caring what the ranchers thought about them. If that made them cattle rustlers, so be it.

The only problem was that in cattle country, rustling is no small offense. Plenty of men had been hanged for it, and they knew they could be too. But someone had to catch them, and the law in Cimarron was not—shall we say—diligent. So while everyone had their suspicions, no one had any proof, and Brad and Will came and went more or less as they pleased.

But because the law was so lax, other outlaws found their way to Cimarron. Gold and copper had been discovered in the mountains nearby, and the area began attracting all manner of loathsome men. Lucien B. Maxwell had created a quiet trading outpost in Cimarron, and around it grew up a friendly mix of Mexican and Anglo families living side-by-side in peace. But outlaws like Clay Allison and Blackjack Ketchum and the serial killer Charlie Kennedy began disturbing that peace. Lucien Maxwell sold out, and the Colfax County War broke out.

The little bit of cattle rustling done by Brad Bradshaw and Will Kane became the least of the town's problems, and one day, some of the men of Cimarron thought Brad and Will might become a solution to those problems.

IV

The four rode steadily on, deeper into the Valle Vidal. Hondo liked one thing about working with Brad Bradshaw most of all: he always planned a smooth getaway. No drama, no breakneck rides. He thought through every angle, every "what if," and he had a plan for it.

The bank in Cimarron was likely full of gold from the Aztec mine up in the Baldy country. Though the high country around Cimarron remained wild, the townspeople bragged that no one had ever robbed the bank and lived to tell about it. Twice before outlaws had tried. The result was seven men dead, all buried in Boot Hill Cemetery on the south edge of town. Brad himself had helped bury the first man, not long after he came into the country.

Every store and office in the town had its rifle or shotgun at hand, and any stranger was under suspicion if he approached the bank. It was the town's bank, and the people of the town intended to protect it. Anyone attempting to rob the Bank of Cimarron must run a gauntlet of rifle fire…in a town notorious for its marksmanship.

They had come to a peculiar feature of the Valle Vidal called the "Wall." It was a rock escarpment with few breaks in it, and they were steep, talus-strewn paths difficult to ride through. Wagons couldn't make it through, and a large posse would have to go through the few breaks in the wall single-file. Or they had to go around—which would take many extra hours. Brad had led them to a spot through the Wall that was the most difficult, and would take the most time to ride around. This, too, was a part of his plan: make the beginning of the pursuit so tough that it broke the horses of the posse. Then mount fresh horses— horses they had hidden in advance—and leave the posse behind.

They rode up a gravel draw, and then up the rocky slide. Near the top they dismounted and horses and riders had to scramble up for themselves. When they got to the top of the wall, they entered the Valle Vidal—the green valley—itself. High mead- ows, some of them with pothole lakes—no more than ponds, really—in the center, often with aspen groves around the edges. They found the makeshift pole corral they had built in a stand of aspens. They turned out the "borrowed" and now exhausted horses they used for the robbery. The horses would find plenty of grass and water in the Valle, and would eventually find their ways back home—or the posse would take them back, if it even got that far.

"Where to now?" Romney asked.

"Rayado," Brad answered. "Then up to Wildhorse Park."

Jeffcoat tilted his hat brim lower. Rayado was on the other side of Cimarron from where they were now. Did Brad have in mind to go through Cimarron, or around it? And what about Will Kane?

V

Back when Will and Brad were running cattle in the Valle Vidal, they were seldom apart, but on one particular day they were.

Will Kane liked being in town more than Brad, so after they had moved Manley Chase's cattle up to pastures high in the Valle Vidal, Will decided he needed a couple of nights at the St. James Hotel in town. Brad would stay with the cows alone, and that was fine with him. The weather was spectacular—cool at night and not too hot in the daytime. Water and plenty of grass. He could babysit the cattle a few days by himself.

It was at the height of Cimarron's troubles. Will had promised Brad he would stay out of that trouble. A couple of whiskeys, a hot bath and a night in a real bed at the St. James, and then back to the Valle Vidal. That was the plan.

Everybody in town knew Will and Brad were selling strays, but only the ranch owners held that against him. Most everybody else half-way admired two young men who didn't have family or connections, working hard to make a few extra dollars. But Will knew that the Big Men in the Cimarron country would waste no misstep he made. It would be all the excuse they needed to send him over to Taos to the judge.

Still, Will was doing okay until a card game in a corner of

the bar got loud. Will could almost smell the trouble coming, so before he could even have that second drink he headed for the door leading into the hotel, where he would pay for a room and go up to bed early.

But two large men blocked his way. Will did not want a fight, so he turned toward the other door, the one that led out into the street. Two more men, not as big, but just as unsavory looking, blocked that path, too.

What happened next is a matter of some speculation. The bar was not well lit, and most of the men in it were drunk. In later years half the population of Colfax County would claim to be in the bar that night, to be an eyewitness, but in truth only about a dozen men and a couple of women of questionable reputation were there, and their stories never quite agreed. Some say the men at the door had called Will a cow thief. Others said no words were spoken. They just wouldn't let Will pass.

All we know for sure is this: before Will Kane could get out the door, guns started flying out of holsters—including a Colt Navy revolver from Will's own. One of the big men by the door raised his gun, but before he could fire Will shot him dead where he stood with the gun in his right hand. He wheeled and fired at one of the men by the other entrance. That man went down, too. When Will looked back at the door, where the big men had stood, the one he hadn't shot was gone. But the man by the other door stood his ground and even got off a shot. However, in the chaos his shot went wild. Will fired again and the man's gun went flying as he grabbed his hand. Will would say later he was not trying to shoot the gun out of the man's hand. "I was just trying to stay alive." Even so, the story spread that Will Kane had shot a gun out of a man's hand rather than kill him.

It was over in seconds. Only then did Will notice that half the chairs and tables in the St. James were turned over, and there was glass scattered all over the floor. A half-dozen men burst into the barroom, some of them with long guns in their hands. One man came forward who identified himself as the mayor and demanded to know what was happening.

Will lowered his gun, and when he was sure these newcomers posed no danger, he held one hand up and slowly put his revolver back in its holster. Four or five men started pointing and talking at once. The mayor lowered his rifle and raised his hand and the room fell silent. He looked around at the chaos and debris and said, "Well, Holy God Almighty."

Then, looking at Will, "Son, did you start this?"

Will looked him in the eye and said with a firm voice, "No, sir. I did not." The mayor walked over to one of the big men slouched in a heap by the door. He had a hole in his chest. There was no doubt: the man was dead.

"Well," the mayor said, "I ought to throw you in jail anyway if for no other reason than you disturbed my evening." It was only then that most of the people in the room noticed that the mayor was wearing nothing but boots, a hat, and long-john underwear. The mayor walked across the room and gently nudged the other dead man with his boot. "But we've got no one to guard you because the man you shot dead here is the same man who shot dead our sheriff last week." The mayor walked over to Will Kane and said, "So I'm not going to throw you in jail. But I am going to tell you not to leave town tomorrow till you come see me. Do you understand me, son?"

"Yes, sir."

"I want to be plain. You have done this town a service by killing these two men, but if you leave town without seeing me tomorrow, I will get a posse together and we will ride up into the Valle Vidal and hunt you and that saddle tramp friend of yours like you were rabid dogs. Am I being plain?"

"Yes, sir. You are. I will come see you in the morning."

"All right," the mayor said, and with an air of such authority that you barely noticed he was wearing nothing but his underwear, the mayor disappeared into the night.

The next morning the mayor asked Will Kane if he wanted to be the sheriff of Cimarron, and in one of those moments that change your life forever, Will Kane said yes and stepped across the line separating the outlaw from the law.

VI

"Are you thinking of knocking over the bank in Cimarron?" Romney asked.

"I might'a been," Brad muttered, but he said nothing more.

Romney did not like the idea, but he only said, "Never was a horse that could not be broke, and never was a rider who couldn't be throwed."

That may be, but that horse could throw a lot of riders before someone finally did ride it.

And the town of Cimarron, with Will Kane for sheriff—well, that was a tough horse for any rider to top off.

Chapter 2

High in the Valle Vidal, between Raton and Taos, is a hidden valley the casual traveler would pass unawares.

If you were traveling south out of La Veta, Colorado, you would cross into New Mexico and you would have to skirt Little Costilla Peak on a high, barely used trail. Continuing south, you would come to a spot on the road of no particular distinction except that a certain notch in the mountain skyline would allow you to look ahead and catch a brief glimpse of Baldy Mountain off in the distance.

The knowing rider would turn off the trail and travel toward that notch.

My father, Dave Stanton, was that knowing rider. And I, a young woman then—a girl, really, just 16 years of age—rode with him.

How we came to be on that trail was a story itself, some of which I will come to in due course, but for now let me simply say that we were riding from Old Colorado City, where my father had lived for several years and where I—after many years of not knowing where he was or even if he was alive—had joined him. We had lived in Old Colorado City through the winter and most of the spring, and now we were headed to California. However, to go west we first needed to go south to the train at Lamy Station, near Santa Fe, and Papa—that's what I called him then and still do—wanted to ride though the high country he loved one last time, and use this last chance to show it to me, too.

We had been on the trail more than a week when we crossed into New Mexico and came to this place. Our goal was to pick our way through the mountains toward Santa Fe. This was not the fastest way—not by a long shot. Nor the safest. Bandits and bears still roamed this high country. And now that the railroad had been finished over Raton Pass and on farther south, we could have taken it all the way from Colorado City to Santa Fe. But Papa knew that the chances of him ever seeing this country again after heading west to California were next to zero.

There was also this: Papa did not talk much, at least not in those days, and we still did not know each other that well. I think my father thought—in the strange way he thought about such things—that the best way for us to get to know each other was to ride this high country together.

So we rode south out of Colorado together, through the Wet Mountains west of Pueblo, through La Veta and over the narrow-gauge railroad that ran into the mining towns farther west. Past the Spanish Peaks, and into New Mexico about forty miles west of Raton Pass.

We rode slowly for several hours after leaving the main trail. The route we took was in such high country that we could pick our way through what little growth there was without any trail to speak of, though our path was cluttered with rocks and sagebrush and scrub oak that caused us to stop many times to look about and pick out our course.

Eventually, though, we came to a narrow canyon, almost a box canyon. We continued uphill as the canyon became narrower, and just as it became so narrow that we could barely fit, we emerged onto the top of a small meadow, with a pond in the middle. Across the meadow we could see rocks that had tumbled off the mountain beyond, littering the edge of the vega.

This little meadow was no more than a small hollow, but it had good grass. A dripping spring on the high side of the meadow fed the small lake. It was a place where several men might remain concealed, unseen even by a rider passing close by, though the place was so remote that few riders ever did come by.

We had come in from the north side of the meadow. But trails led out in other directions. Headed southwest was the trail we would take, past Elizabethtown and Wildhorse Park and beyond, eventually all the way to Santa Fe, and then to Lamy Station, not far from Santa Fe, and the train to California.

I am an old woman now—much older than my father was on that day, but to me, then, he looked old and tired beyond description. I will say, though, that when we came to this high mountain meadow—he simply called it High Park—his countenance brightened. This was a place he knew as a place of peace. Back in the day, when he was a young trapper and miner and occasional cowboy, this was a place to which he would retreat. Seeing it again brought those pleasant memories flooding back.

We drew rein at the edge of the meadow. I knew this is where we would spend the night when I saw him pull out his tobacco and start building a cigarette. His horse also relaxed as Papa gave him his head. The pony started munching on the thick green grass at its feet.

After a few seconds he said, "There's a spring behind that tree."

"Papa," I said. "It's lovely. It really is."

He was silent for a few seconds, as if a statement so obvious and true did not need a response. It just needed to hang in the air and spread out over the meadow.

"Jump down and see if you can get us a fire started," he said. "I could use some coffee. There should be enough stuff just lying around for that, but I'll go fetch us some proper wood."

Papa walked over to where a large boulder sat at the edge of the meadow. I noticed words scratched into the rock:

Near here lies
Bert Carnavon
Dead by the gun
1866

"Did you know that man?" I asked.

"I did," Papa said. "He was an outlaw, and Ali I'm ashamed to tell you that, not so many years ago, I rode with Carnie. That's what we called him. It was right when the war ended and I had come out West trying to outrun what the war had done to me."

He paused for a few seconds, taking a long draw on his cigarette, and then continued.

"But I realized two things. First, you can't outrun yourself, and second, I was no outlaw. It didn't take me long to realize my mistake, and I broke it off and found honest work up in Colorado, and then headed back east. I got as far back as Ft. Worth when I met your mother. Before that happened, though, I made a second mistake: I showed Carnie this place. And a year or so after I stopped riding with him he had gotten himself into some trouble. I don't even remember what now, but he ended up leading a posse up here and they shot him dead."

As I heard my father tell this tale every brain cell in my head was firing. It was as if I was getting a glimpse into a life my father had lived but had—so far—worked hard to keep from me. Was this why we were taking this way to Santa Fe? Maybe he hadn't been trying to hide all this from me. Maybe he just wanted to tell me in the only way he knew how, and the only way I had a chance of actually understanding, by riding along some of the same trails he had ridden.

But I didn't fully understand then. In fact, I must have shown some confusion on my face as I tried to fit these acts of violence into the picture I had of him. Papa saw the confusion.

"Maybe I shouldn't have told you that," he said.

"No, Papa. It's okay. It's just…. Did you carve these words?"

"I did. I wasn't here when they shot Carnie, and I heard they had just left him up here. I really don't know where. We may be standing on him now."

That thought gave me a shudder…but also a flush of excitement.

"Anyway, I thought there ought to be some remembrance of him, so I wrote what you see there. I didn't have any proper tools for the job, so you can barely read it now. A few fading words is not much to account for a man's life, but I figure even an outlaw deserves at least that."

He picked up some deadfall branches and broke off some dead, sap-soaked root from a fallen spruce—lighter-stump that took right away to a match. I quickly got a fire started. Papa shot a couple of fat rabbits. Before long it was dark, but we were warm and cozy and full and sipping coffee by the fire.

"Papa, will we have neighbors where we're going, in California?"

"I expect we will," he said. "It's not a wilderness there anymore. They've got real towns and farms and ranches and even churches, I expect."

"Like back East?"

"Yes, like back East." Then, after a beat: "No, not like back East, exactly. At least I hope not like back East."

I knew what he was thinking, or at least I thought I did. As I said, for a year or two after the war things had not gone well for him. But he must have known what I was thinking, too.

"Yes, we'll have neighbors in California. I'll make sure of it."

For those few years after mother died, Papa "lost his head" as he would later say. First the war, and then this. He once told me he never stopped believing in God, but for a few years he thought God was mad at him and, he said, "I was damn sure mad at him."

Plus, after what he had done in the war, he said, he thought God might have good reason. He said he thought he was cursed, and many times, he said, he thought I would be better without him.

"When I was in the war they would tell us not to bunch up," he said. "So one canister won't kill us all at once. So I got to thinking after the war: What if I am cursed? If I am, I wasn't doing anyone any favors to be around them. I thought during those days that I was hurting you more than helping you to be around you."

I was just a baby then and remember none of it. We had mother's family around us then, in Ft. Worth, and when Mama died, they took me in while Papa worked first in the stockyards and then rode with a couple of outfits up the Chisholm Trail to Kansas, and then west into Colorado, down into New Mexico. He just disappeared for a few years—more than a few years, really.

But he eventually came back to Ft. Worth. I was in school by then, and had been for some years. My mother's family wasn't wealthy, exactly, but they had money enough, so they sent me to school back East. They said it was for the best. If I stayed in Ft. Worth, I would be the girl whose mother was dead and whose father had gone bad. Back East, in boarding school, none of the girls had family nearby. We were all away from home. In a strange way, they were right: it had been for the best.

Though it took me years to understand that.

II

When we were up in Colorado City, Papa was constantly saying it wasn't right for a man to keep his daughter in a shack in a frontier town. He would say I needed to meet decent folks, to learn things from other women. I know what he really meant was that I needed to meet some decent men, and in Colorado City that seemed unlikely to happen. That, too, was a part of the reason he had decided to light out for California.

But the truth is that I liked Colorado City—they call it Colorado Springs today. Yes, it was a rough town with plenty of rough men, but I guess I had already come to believe that there were not "good" men or "bad" men. There were just men, and the line between good and evil runs through the heart of us all.

I think Papa believed that, too. Years later, Papa was fond of saying, "I trust all men. It's the devil inside 'em I don't trust." He would always laugh as he said it, but he believed it.

In any case, after we ate a bite, I asked Papa about the man buried in this meadow.

"Carnie was a decent man. He was no angel, mind you, or he would have never ended up where he did. But he was decent enough. Courteous to women. Skilled with a gun, which takes some discipline and practice, and that's always a virtue in this country.

"But sometimes you can be too quick, and that's what happened to Carnie. He had gotten into a card game in Taos and it soon became obvious the other guy was cheating, so Carnie called him on it. It was a foolish thing to do. He should have just gotten up from the table and walked away, but—like I said—Carnie was a decent man and in his mind cheating was something he could not abide."

Papa paused. He pulled a bandana out of his pocket and leaned in toward the fire and used the bandana as a hotpad to grab the coffee pot. He poured himself another cup and leaned back out of the light. His face was in darkness as he continued.

"So the cheater drew on Carnie but—like I said—Carnie was quick with a gun and killed the cheater with one shot. A dozen men in the bar saw what happened. It could not have been plainer that the cheater had drawn first and that Carnie had to fire just to defend himself.

"But what Carnie didn't know was that the little hot-headed cheater was the son of a big man, part owner of one of the mines near Elizabethtown, just west of here. So the next day the sheriff came looking for Carnie. And Carnie lost his head and ran, and that just made everyone who wasn't in the saloon that night jump to the conclusion that Carnie was guilty.

"Anyway. They caught him here, and it was then that I quit this country and rode north to Colorado City, stopping by here along the way. That's when I carved what you saw there on the rock."

III

I was snuggled as far down in my blankets as I could. Papa scattered the sticks in the fire so it still glowed but did not put off any flames. I stared up at the sky through the ponderosa pine and fir trees until I could no longer keep my eyes open.

I do not know how much later it was when I opened my eyes again, but something told me it was near dawn, because I could now see a half-moon, partly hidden by the trees, but high in the sky. Only a few coals remained of the fire. Something had startled me to awareness, but I didn't know what yet. I lay perfectly still. Listening.

At first I heard only the water from the spring, trickling, but then I began to make out something else.

Riders.

"Papa?" I said.

"I hear them," he whispered. Then, after a few seconds, "Get dressed and stand over by the horses."

I wriggled into my pants under the blankets. In a wink I was dressed and quietly moved over to where we had hobbled the horses. They nuzzled up to me and I put my hand on them gently to reassure them, to keep them quiet and still.

From where we were, in the trees on the high side of the meadow, we had a good view of the trail. I had no trouble seeing them in the light of the half-moon.

Four riders.

The way they were slumped in their saddles, I imagined immediately they must have been traveling all night. Something seemed familiar about the second man in the saddle, something about the bulk of his huge body.

Hondo. Papa had ridden with him in his outlaw days, and once—up in Colorado City—I had met him. More than met him. Papa had found work there as a carpenter and handyman, and when he had saved enough money, he sent for me. During the time we were in Colorado City I got to meet some of the men there, and I remembered Hondo in particular. He was a big man, good with his hands, who would occasionally work with Papa on some of the construction jobs. I would bring Papa lunch and sometimes supper, and Papa introduced us. Once, when Hondo wasn't around, Papa told me that the big man had been an outlaw back in the day, and that I should stay away from him.

So, yes, I remembered Hondo, and this was Hondo, sure enough. And since I am being candid, and writing this story by way of a confession, I must confess that even though Papa had told me to stay away from him, all that did was make me more curious, so I noticed him every time I saw him. I knew Papa was trying to protect me, but I liked Hondo. He may have been an outlaw, but he was not a mean man.

As I rubbed my hand over the horses, they stayed calm and quiet, but the sorrel must have caught a whiff of the riders or their horses. The horse whinnied, and that was all it took. The four riders, without a word, scattered from the middle of the meadow to the shadows of the trees around its edge.

Papa grabbed his rifle and crouched, waiting. I grabbed my rifle from its scabbard and slid behind a boulder that would provide me a measure of protection while still giving me a good view of the meadow.

The sky began to brighten, and then something surprising happened. The man I would soon learn was Brad Bradshaw called, "I'm coming out. Don't shoot me, now."

He stepped out into the open—but not where I thought he would be. I spun sharply and pointed my rifle at him, but he was already facing me. His hands were in the air, but he had not dropped his own rifle. He held it over his head in his right hand.

"It's all right," he said. "I'm friendly."

"Well don't get too friendly," I said.

Brad told me later that it was in that moment that he fell in love with me because in that moment, he said, I was excited, but not afraid. And he liked that I looked like I might actually know how to use the rifle.

He was right about me being able to use the rifle. Papa had made sure of that. But the rest was romantic nonsense, I would tell him. I was plenty afraid.

From behind Brad came a voice, Hondo's voice. "Dave Stanton. It's Hondo. We're coming out."

Papa was ten yards away, behind another boulder. He looked over at me and smiled, shaking his head in disbelief—and relief. Keeping his gun at the ready, he walked out from behind the boulder and stepped across the meadow toward Brad and Hondo, who himself had stepped out of the trees.

Hondo turned his head. "Come on in, boys. I know this old

rawhide."

I followed Papa out from behind the rocks, keeping a wary eye on Brad, who was in turn looking hard at me.

"Did you hear that?" he said. "We're friends. Hondo knows your Pa."

"My Pa," I said, "knows a lot of folks. And we know Hondo, though I don't know I would exactly call him a friend."

"What the hell..." Hondo said, in mock indignation. He shot me a hard glance, and then looked at Papa, who let out a laugh.

Brad smiled. "Yes. I reckon that's true enough. But either way, what do you say we both lower our guns and try to sort this unexpected meeting out together."

Chapter 3

"He's all right," Hondo said, looking past me at Papa. "I rode with Stanton. And we worked together up in Colorado City for a spell." Everyone relaxed. Brad and I both lowered our guns. Hondo gestured toward Papa.

"Dave Stanton, meet Brad Bradshaw."

Papa walked past me toward Brad. I followed behind Papa. Brad met us in the middle of the meadow. It was fully light now, and the meadow was damp with dew.

"I reckon I've heard a story or two about you, Bradshaw," Papa said, who motioned for me to come up alongside him.

"Hondo's told us a bit about you, too," Brad said.

Romney and Jeffcoat came out of the trees and stood some distance behind Hondo, who was behind Brad.

Papa spoke: "This is Ali. Alison, but we call her Ali. She's my daughter. We're headed to California, though we've got to get to Santa Fe and Lamy Station first. Then we'll take the train west."

I could see Brad and the other men sizing up Papa. My father had always been larger than life to me. Up until then, I had thought of him as a giant, but for the first time that morning I saw him through the eyes of someone else, through the eyes of these much younger men, and I suddenly saw my father as an old man. He was quick-witted and had bright eyes, to be sure. But he was also slope-shouldered, with worn clothes, an unruly beard, and thinning hair.

Still, I could hear the respect in Hondo's voice, and I could also see Brad showing him some deference. They may have seen his age and even some weakness, but they also saw a man who had survived many years in rough country, a man saddle-hardened and trail-wise. Not someone to underestimate.

"And, boys, this is that beautiful daughter I was telling you about," Hondo said.

Romney, a wiry man with a quick step, came forward, followed by Jeffcoat, the Indian. Both of them put their hands to their hats and nodded their heads slightly in that way a cowboy greets a woman. Romney spoke first.

"Hondo, you are so full of tall tales and exaggeration that I never knew what to believe of all your stories, but I must say you were telling the truth about this one. She's as pretty as you said she was."

I must have blushed. I know my eyes fell to the ground. Papa put his arm around me, looked Bradshaw in the eye, and said, "She's very special to me."

It was a terribly sweet thing for a father to say, but it was also a warning, and the other men in the meadow understood that plainly.

"Going to marry her off to some farmer?" Hondo asked.

"She ain't going to marry no outlaw, if that's what you mean." Papa glanced at Brad.

The four men let that hang in the air for a second, but Hondo quickly broke the tension. "What are y'all doing way up here? Why didn't you just take the train down to Lamy?"

"Well," Papa began, with a bit of hesitation in his voice. "I thought I'd show Ali this country one last time before we headed to California."

"Fair enough," Brad said. "But this is still pretty wild country for an…for one man and a young girl." Brad caught himself before he said "an old man."

"We're doin' all right so far," Papa said. "What are you boys doing way up here and where are you headed?"

More awkward silence.

Papa smiled, knowing the answer even before he asked the question.

"The Valle Vidal is a good place to stay hid for a while, but if I was you boys, I would stay away from Cimarron."

Hondo took the bait. "I reckon we'll go where we want."

"Not if you're riding with him," Papa nodded at Brad.

"You don't know Brad," Hondo snapped back.

"I know Will Kane," Papa said. "And Bradshaw does too." Papa looked over at Brad.

"That's true enough," Brad said. "I do know Will Kane. We used to ride together all through this country." Brad tipped his hat back and sized up Papa. "You don't miss much, do you, old man?" Only this time the use of the word "old" was one of respect.

"I hear things," Papa said. "But I don't say much. So if you boys go your way and let us go ours, I reckon there won't be trouble for either of us."

It was well light now, and though these four riders seemed friendly enough, it was pretty clear they were fleeing trouble and heading toward more trouble. In short, not good traveling companions.

"Fair enough," Brad said again.

I brought up our horses. The man they called Jeffcoat, the Indian, brought Brad's horse out of the woods. They all filled their canteens in the spring, mounted swiftly and silently, and rode south out of the meadow, toward Cimarron. Though when Brad got to the edge of the meadow, he wheeled his horse around expertly, looked me straight in the eye, and raised his hand to his hat—the cowboy's salute.

I blushed again, and Papa saw it.

"Stay away from men like that, Ali. They're no good."

"They didn't seem so bad," I said. "And wasn't Hondo your friend?"

"He was." Then Papa's voice softened as he said, "I guess he still is. He's a hard worker. And there's not a cruel bone in his body. Not like that Romney, a real hothead. Anyway, Hondo never caught a break with the law, and that made him angry and…not mean, but sad. Hondo might've made a good rancher if things had broke a little different for him.

"And Bradshaw? Well, everybody knows his story. A raw deal all the way around. To be honest, I'm amazed he's turned out as good as he has. I've known men who had a much better go of it turn out a whole lot meaner. Don't get me wrong. I'm not justifying his bank robbin'. But I think I can see his side of it, too."

Papa turned to his horse. He patted the pony's neck, and checked the cinch. It wasn't so long ago that Papa was riding with men like that. He had told me some of the stories, but they were not stories he told readily, or with much fondness. Long and cold rides. Lonely camps. Often little to eat.

That's why we were headed to California. It was a land of "milk and honey," Papa was fond of saying. I think he knew it wasn't true, but he liked the sound of it.

I could not help but notice one thing, and I swallowed hard before I said it out-loud.

"He's handsome, Papa. The tall one, I mean. Bradshaw."

"I was afraid you might think that. But daughter of mine, men like that bring the women in their lives nothing but grief. I understand the attraction. Hell, I even like Bradshaw myself. And maybe one day—if he isn't shot by a faster hand, or doesn't die of the cold one night, or isn't caught and hanged for what he's already done—well, maybe one day he'll ride out of this country and end up some place nobody knows him and make a new start."

"Like California?"

Papa let that sink in for a moment. "Well, maybe."

We both pulled ourselves into our saddles and settled in. Papa looked toward the south, toward the trail Brad's gang took toward Cimarron.

"But I'm afraid Brad Bradshaw has more than hard country between him and California."

II

Brad proved Papa's words by heading to Cimarron. Will Kane would not arrest him on sight. No one had seen them rob the bank in Raton. Because of Brad's clever horse swap, no one even knew what they were riding. That's the way it had been everywhere he went. He would show up in a country, and a bank would get robbed, and he would disappear, but no one ever caught him doing the robbing, or ever even caught him with the money.

So Will Kane would let him ride into town. In fact, he might even be glad to see him—or at least not angry to see him. After all, things had turned out pretty well for Will. He no longer slept out in the cold. He had a house, and a respectable job as sheriff, and he even had a pretty young wife.

It was riding out of town that might prove harder. The Bank of Cimarron had a safe, full of gold, that had never been cracked. It was a temptation too much for Brad Bradshaw. And, of course, it wasn't just that. Kane had stolen from Bradshaw the only thing—the only person, at least till I came along—he had really ever loved. Will Kane had built a life with her, and a big part of what he valued now was his reputation as sheriff. To crack the safe of the Cimarron Bank—well, it was a way to get back at Will, to get back at the town of Cimarron, to get back at all those who had been so quick to push him over the line to the wrong side of the law, and then hate him for being there.

Papa and I, on the other hand, had our eyes set on California. Papa said he knew where we were going. It was a little town called Pasadena, tucked in a corner of the San Gabriel Valley on the edge of the mountains, about 20 miles in from the coast. Some years earlier he laid up there several months when he had wanted to be out of sight. Like the Valle Vidal, it too was a place of peace for Papa. He wanted to go there again.

Since I had fled boarding school and joined Papa last year, he had taken only honest work. No more outlawing. But we both needed a fresh start. Since Papa hadn't been spending his money on liquor, or just gambling it away or plain losing it after going on long drunks, he had been able to save a few dollars. More than a few, really. He would sometimes say, "It's amazing how fast the money piles up if you work hard and don't set a match to it."

So with the money Papa had been able to save, we planned to buy a little place from the Indians or the Mexicans or whomever was selling in Pasadena. We would irrigate a patch, and grow fruit trees, or vegetables, or maybe both.

But first we had to get to Santa Fe, and the train station at Lamy, just south of Santa Fe. And we had a week of beautiful but rough trail riding ahead of us. So while Brad and his men turned due south toward Cimarron, we headed southwest toward Elizabethtown, then almost due south and down the length of Moreno Valley to Wildhorse Park, which was 20 miles south of Cimarron. Then we'd head into the high country of the Pecos wilderness toward Santa Fe.

If we didn't run into any bad weather, or outlaws, or other kind of trouble, we would make the train in a week. Ten days at the most. And to California a week after that.

But as we rode across the high country of the Valle Vidal, it seemed a dream too fantastic to hope for. So I didn't. I just kept both eyes on the trail, and one hand resting on the butt of my pistol as we rode along.

"And if anybody asks," Papa said, "we didn't see anybody. You don't know nothing about nothing."

"Yessir."

III

Papa was alert as we rode. This was never exactly Indian country. The Spanish and the Mexicans had been here for hundreds of years. But it was remote country. It was where bad men went—Indian, or Mexican, or white—when people were chasing them. It had plenty of places to hide until folks stopped chasing.

So there was no telling who or what we might run into.

I knew even then that Papa was taking something of a chance having me along. But it was the only chance either of us had, really. Back East, I was an orphan, or the daughter of an outlaw. I had gotten a pretty good education, and likely could have found a job as a teacher. Maybe I was foolish, because that would not have been a bad life—back in Ft. Worth, teaching, perhaps marrying a shop owner.

All I can say is that it was not the life I wanted. So I wrote Papa at an address I had for him in Colorado City, and—well, it's a story too long to tell except to say that eventually he got the letter. He sent me enough money to buy a train ticket to Denver. I wrote Papa back that very day and bought a ticket within the week. Papa met me at the Denver station with a horse. We rode south along the Front Range until we got to Colorado City, and settled there through the fall and winter. Come spring we started making our plans to leave this country for good. I remember the day he first spoke our plans out loud.

"We could ride north to Cheyenne on a good road and take the Union Pacific from there all the way to California," he said. "But I would like to see this country one last time, if you're willing."

"Sure, Papa," I said. "I'm with you, now."

So we would head south instead, and take the mountain route. By the time we had run across Brad and his men, we had been on the trail for more than a week. We had crossed the Wet Mountains west of Pueblo. Sierra Blanca towered to the southwest. Then across the Arkansas River and through La Veta Pass into New Mexico. It was the wildest and most beautiful country I had ever seen.

Papa rode a few yards in front of me, Winchester in hand. This was not the wild and lawless country it had been ten or twenty years earlier, but there was still plenty out there that could hurt you—even kill you. Between mountain lions and bears and bad men, you had to stay alert.

And, unlike Brad and his gang, Papa had no desire to go through Cimarron. Somebody might remember his connections with Hondo and assume that whatever mischief Hondo had been a part of he had been a part of, too.

So as nice as it might have been to sleep in a bed, or get a meal that someone else cooked, we rode around Cimarron in a wide circle. We never let the town even come into view. We continued west toward Questa, but we turned south before we got there, traveling through the high country to Bobcat Pass, along the western shoulder of Baldy Mountain, and then south into Moreno Valley. We would make good time through Moreno Valley before heading up in the high country again, to Wildhorse Park. We would find a store there, a trading post and an inn with beds, and we could rest up and buy some supplies before making the final push to Santa Fe.

The sun came up over the ridge and it grew hot. Nothing moved. Papa kept his eyes on the horizon and on the ground in front of us, and after a while he saw what he had been worried about: the tracks of four unshod ponies. Not Brad and his boys. In fact, it was impossible to say who they were. All we knew was they crossed the trail we were on, but almost at right angles, headed east. Papa looked off to the left. We could see for a half-mile or so before the trail disappeared over a ridge, but we saw no one. The tracks were fresh, no more than a couple of hours old. Whoever had made them was up in those hills, maybe even looking at us now. But we could see nothing. If they were out there, they didn't want to be seen.

We rode for the rest of the day and spent another night out under the stars near Bobcat Pass. To the south Moreno Valley spread out before us for thirty miles or more—ringed by mountains on all sides.

"It's beautiful, Papa," I said for what may have been the hundredth time on this trip. It seemed that every hour had brought a new and marvelous sight. We made fast time downhill from Bobcat Pass into the valley itself. We passed Elizabethtown, a mining village, without even stopping, and then south on a wide wagon road that ran the length of the long, grassy high country park. About halfway down Moreno Valley we turned east. After almost a full day of gentle downhill, we went steeply uphill again. We were headed toward Wildhorse Park.

It was high above Moreno Valley, south and west of Cimarron. It's a huge, 10,000-acre meadow in the sky, with a swale in the middle. In wet years a pond formed there that sometimes swelled to the size of a lake—Wildhorse Lake.

A mile north of the lake in a stand of aspen trees, there was a small store, wagon stop, and saloon owned by Rye Burns. In his younger days Burns was an up-and-coming lawyer in Texas, and had even been a judge for a while. But his love for rye whiskey gave him a nickname and cost him his job. He drifted west and eventually settled on the edge of Wildhorse Park, providing a way station for those who turned off the Santa Fe Trail at Rayado and headed west toward Taos.

The store building was eighty feet long and twenty feet wide. It was built of adobe, and facing it across what was humorously called the "plaza"—an expanse of hard-packed dirt—was another building almost identical in size which was a bunkhouse carrying a faded sign: "Beds—Two Bits."

A funny thing happened to Rye Burns at Wildhorse Park: he stopped drinking and those who knew him during those years say he appeared to grow younger. By the time we passed through in that summer of 1881, he was no longer the stooped man Papa said we would find there. I found him to be a tall, vaguely handsome man in a world-weary way, a man who still carried himself with the somewhat regal bearing of the judge he once was.

Not much happened in Colfax or Taos Counties that Rye Burns did not know about. Maybe it was his legal training, I don't know, but Burns was a man who listened well and had found ways to profit from the information he gathered. And even when he was a drunk—perhaps because he was a drunk, who knows—he was a man who had many times proved his courage against the Apaches, although these days the Indians, as I said, had mostly settled down to be farmers or were far away on a reservation somewhere.

That's not to say that Rye Burns was a paragon of virtue. Far from it. He would sell whiskey to drunks and bullets to outlaws and shovels to undertakers, all with equal aplomb.

But Rye Burns, now sober, did retain one virtue. He knew when to keep his mouth shut.

IV

After they left Papa and me up in the Valle Vidal, Brad Bradshaw and his boys had gone toward Cimarron, but they had not gone into town. They paused on a ridge just north of town, on old Manley Chase's ranch, and looked down on the village. It was a place Brad knew because he and Will Kane used to pause there. It offered an expansive view of the town. Sometimes they would even camp there. One time Brad told Will, "Someday I'm going to build a hacienda here and call it 'Casa del Corazon,'"— Spanish for 'Home of the Heart.'

Will just laughed at that.

"You go right ahead," he said. "As for me, I'm going to leave this town as quick as I'm able. I would like to see the Pacific Ocean before I die."

Brad remembered that conversation as he and the boys paused on that peaceful spot overlooking town. And he could not help but note that things had not turned out as either of them had planned. After he pulled off this job, Brad would never be able to come to Cimarron again. And Will, who wanted to leave this town forever and see the Pacific Ocean—well, he was dug in sure enough. A sheriff and a family man. He wasn't going anywhere.

Brad pointed to the town below, spread out in front of them like a toy model. He showed the boys where the bank was, and pointed out where to cross the Cimarron River headed south toward Rayado, and where the sheriff's office was, and—well, where everything was that they needed to know in order to rob the bank in a few days.

Then they rode wide around the town, and south around an old Santa Fe Trail landmark called the Tooth of Time. Once they cleared the Tooth, they turned west into the mountains, past Lover's Leap and over a high pass before dropping down toward the Rayado River. They rode up river until they got to the headwaters, and then finally south to Rye Burns' place at Wildhorse

Park.

The porch in front of the store offered a good view both up and down the trail, while behind the place to the north were towering ridges that led up to Clear Creek Mountain and—farther beyond—to Baldy Mountain, where the gold and silver and copper mines were located. Burns was standing in his doorway when Brad led his small cavalcade into the plaza, where they dismounted and tied their horses.

"I was wondering when I was going to see you," Burns said.

Brad smiled and nodded at Burns, but otherwise ignored him. Brad glanced all around. He told me later that he had been vaguely disappointed I wasn't there, and more than a little worried, given all the dangers in the country. Given his own outlaw status there was, of course, a certain irony in that. Besides, even though we were in fact headed to Wildhorse Park, the route we took—through high country before dropping into Moreno Valley—would not get us there as quickly as Brad and his gang.

Hondo by now could almost tell what was on Brad's mind. He dismounted and walked over to him.

"Don't worry about them, Bradshaw. Dave Stanton's no fool. They'll be fine."

Jeffcoat led his horse to the trough for water, and then to the corral.

"You're probably right," Brad said. "But, you know, Hondo, worry is what I do."

Hondo nodded. "I know that's true." Then, after a beat, "Brad, I've never seen or heard of anybody better. You've robbed a dozen banks in this country and nobody even knows your name. Except for Cimarron, you could ride into any town in Colorado or New Mexico and no one would be the wiser—except for those who have ridden with you.

"But you know you ain't cut out for this, no matter how good you are at it. I never knew a man who was less cut out for it. To me this comes natural and easy, but not for you. The very thing that makes you good at this business shows you don't belong in it. You've got an instinct to watch out for the other fellow. You don't care how much grief you shoulder yourself as long as you can keep others out of trouble. That's why you plan so carefully. That's why you're worrying about Stanton and that girl now."

"Maybe."

He glanced around at Burns. "You been to Cimarron lately?"

"No," Burns said. "Not lately. Two weeks ago. Maybe three."

"So no news?"

Burns smiled. "Oh, well, you know. Riders come through, so we still get a bit of news."

"Like what?" Brad was fishing to find out what Burns knew.

"Like the Bank of Raton got robbed," Burns said. "And nobody has the vaguest idea who did it."

Burns rubbed his hands together and smiled, like a card player who could not wait for the next hand to deal. He turned to go inside. Brad followed. Brad and Burns understood each other. They were both talented men. Both had been dealt one too many bad hands in a row before they figured out the game was rigged against them. And both of them were now trying to take back what they had been cheated out of.

And not only did they understand each other, they each had something they could hold over the other. Take Burns. He was only too happy to do business with men others would not. An outlaw could stop off at Wildhorse Park, buy supplies, pick up information, and never worry about anything being said. It was a safe place—as safe as any man living beyond the law could find.

And one of the things Burns knew was that Brad Bradshaw had robbed the bank in Raton. It was too well planned. They had gotten away too cleanly. It had to be Bradshaw, Burns knew. Burns also knew they hadn't gotten away with much. And from those two facts he could guess they now had their sights set on Cimarron.

But Burns also knew Will Kane and—truth be told—he liked the man. Burns may have been operating on the edge of the law himself, but he had been careful not to cross completely over the line. And a lot of the supplies Burns sold came from Cimarron. In short, what was good for Cimarron was good for Rye Burns, at least most of the time. But a lot of Burns' supplies came from other places, and that was good for Cimarron, too. The Maxwell Land Grant Company, and its Cattle Company, owned Cimarron, so having Burns—a resourceful man who was able to get things, to do things—well, that had its advantages for folks on both sides of the law.

Inside the saloon, Burns poured Brad a drink. With only Brad and his men around, Burns spoke freely.

"It's your business," Burns said. "But have you thought this through?"

Brad clinched his jaw to keep the irritation welling up in him from showing on his face.

"If I hadn't thought this through, would we be here now? Would we be having this conversation?"

Burns nodded. He had a point.

"So what do you need from me?"

"I want to know what's in the bank, and how long it will be there."

"How am I supposed to find that out?" Burns said.

"The same way you find out everything else."

Burns wanted to smile, because he knew Brad was giving him a compliment, but he caught himself. Yes, he could find out, but he didn't want Brad to know how, or that it was easy. Rye Burns knew that his value to men like Brad was that what he did seemed a lot like magic.

"All right," Burns said. "I'm heading down to Cimarron now. I won't be back till tomorrow morning. You boys make yourself at home."

"And we'll need horses, too. Four of them. And we'll need our horses tied up at Lookout Meadow."

"That will not be a problem."

If Burns was worried about what he had just agreed to do— to aid and abet the robbery of the Cimarron Bank—he did not let on. He must have known, though, that what he had done carried with it some risk. If the bank in Cimarron had as much money in it as everyone said it did—from the Aztec mine up in the Baldy country—this robbery would be a big score. Will Kane couldn't just let it pass. And neither would the town. And if they didn't catch Brad, the mining company or the insurance company would likely bring in the Pinkertons.

It dawned on Burns what Brad was doing. This was the Main Chance. Brad was aiming for one last score so big that he would never have to rob banks again. This was his ticket out of the out-law life. If he could rob the bank and no one knew it was him, he could take from this country what it had taken from him. He would get his life back.

But if he didn't pull it off, he would hang.

What Burns had to make sure of was this: that he didn't hang, too.

V

Brad used to tell me that being a bank robber was the best possible training for being a movie producer. It was true. Both required planning and cunning. A razor's edge separated success and failure. More than that, in the movie business, a grand-slam home run could set you up for life. Or you could fail so spectacularly in the movie business that it was impossible to recover.

But that wisdom came later. On that day at Wildhorse Park, Brad was just trying to figure out every angle, to hold it all in his head, and to put in place an alternative plan for every possible contingency.

Cimarron had changed since he and Will Kane had raised hell there as younger men. There were families there now. Will Kane himself had a family. A beautiful young wife named Sydney—a young woman Brad once had his eye on himself, or so I found out much later.

There must be no killing. Brad wanted to rob the bank in Cimarron to get the money and to taunt them. No, more than taunt them, to take back from them what they had taken from him. But he wanted no killing. To begin with, he hated no one there. But, secondly, there was a practical consideration. If you take someone's money, they will come after you, but only for a while. At some point the cost of a chase becomes greater than the value of what you're chasing, in time, money, and loneliness. But if Brad or his gang killed a man in Cimarron, that man would be someone's husband, or father, or son, or friend—and the chase would never be over—it would continue world without end.

So no killing.

Brad had also noticed that the men in the posse rarely had money in the banks. They rode for the reward, and for the adventure. But if the chase turned into days, the reward was rarely worth it. And heaven knows the sport goes out of the chase soon enough. After the first missed meal, perhaps, and certainly after the first night on the cold, hard ground.

So, no, there would be no killing. Just a good plan, and enough money to ride out of the country in style.

In Spanish, *cimarron* means 'wild one,' and the town had lived up to its name many times. The St. James Hotel in Cimarron still had bullet holes in the ceiling, put there by the gunfighter Clay Allison. In fact, some say that Clay Allison left the Cimarron country and went back to Texas because of Will Kane. That seems unlikely, though Clay Allison was a complicated man and it is hard to say. All we know for sure about Allison is that after he was married and his first daughter was born in Cimarron, he soon moved away, and that was about the time Will Kane became sheriff and the town settled down to a relatively quiet respectability.

Will Kane also settled down to a life of respectability. The town needed someone who was tough enough, perhaps even bad enough, to get the job done. Kane needed a way out of the outlaw's life. In some ways the deal Kane cut with Cimarron was a desperate solution for both the sheriff and the town. Being sheriff of a town like Cimarron was not soft duty. Kane could just as easily have ended up dead. And if Kane did not prove to be the right man, Cimarron's lawlessness would have driven people away, and the town would become one of the thousands of ghost towns that dot the American West.

But if it did work, Kane would just be a man with a past that no one spoke of, and the town would survive.

And that may be why Brad was so set on robbing the bank in Cimarron. It was Brad who Kane and the town threw under the coach. Sure, Brad and Kane had rustled a little cattle, had broken a few laws, but they had been young men, and they had done nothing people couldn't forget if they were given other things to remember. But when the town recruited Kane as sheriff, they gave him a badge, a salary, and a place to live. Alright, so it was a lean-to addition on the back of the town jail, but it had a solid bed, and a stove, and a roof that didn't leak. And just about every night he'd be invited to dinner in someone's home, or one of the women of the town would show up in the late afternoon with enough food not only for the night, but to take the edge off the next morning, too.

And after everything Kane had endured as a cowboy and a rustler, in those first weeks it felt like living in a mansion.

But here was the catch: it was temporary. To make the arrangement permanent, Kane had to bring the cattle rustling to an end. Kane and Brad both knew this assignment would put them on a collision course. If Brad had stayed in Colfax County, he would have had to kill Will Kane, or Will Kane would have had to kill him. Leaving was the only way to untangle the knot.

But then gold was discovered in the high country and the Aztec Mine brought all manner of men to the country. Cimarron, for a season, boomed. Will Kane not only had respectability, but a real town to rule over. After Clay Allison rode back east to Texas, the town had become almost citified, quiet. Families came, though some of them became squatters on the Maxwell Land Grant, which set off problems of its own. Still, Kane seemed up to any and all challenges.

That's why Brad grinned to himself at the thought of outwitting Will Kane and carrying off the robbery.

Brad also reflected on the fact that Will Kane was the only man who had ever whipped him in a fist-fight. Despite the fact that they had been close friends, they had also been young men, and they sometimes fought like brothers.

Brad remembered the last fight they had before he left Cimarron for Colorado. Will Kane was somewhat heavier, but a fast man for his weight, and he was no quitter. Many years later Brad could remember the details of that day. Will had been in Cimarron a few weeks and it was becoming clear that he was winning Sydney's affections. Late one afternoon at the bar of the St. James, Brad told Will Kane that Sydney could never love men like them.

Will, though, had already come to believe that maybe, just maybe, and against all odds, he could win a woman like Sydney.

Brad had teased him: "What would she see in a couple of saddle tramps like us?" But Will Kane was already planning his future, and that future meant as few people in Cimarron as possible knowing his past. The words became heated, and before long fists started flying.

And Kane had whipped him.

Brad, in his quiet moments, replayed the fight in his head, and he wondered if in some way he wanted to be beaten. Rather, if he didn't feel like he deserved to be beaten for all the bad things he had done. Maybe if he let Will Kane beat him, it would somehow make amends, it would somehow be his penance.

And even though it was a foolish and childish thing to wish for, Brad sometimes wished for one more chance to fight Kane.

But there would be no time for that. They would have to plan this one with infinite care.

Unless…. What if he could make a fight a part of the plan?

VI

Rye Burns' store smelled of dry goods, of calico and gingham, of new leather and gun oil, of tobacco and spices. There was a rack of new Winchesters, a couple of second-hand Spencers, a case containing some new six-shooters, and the usual odds and ends of gear and supplies to be found around any frontier trading post.

Hondo cut off a piece of cheese with his jack-knife and walked over to where Brad was seated. He hitched himself up on a barrel.

"It should be rich," Hondo said, abruptly bringing the conversation to the safe in Cimarron. "But it's a tough one."

Brad was a planner, but Hondo was a bit of a planner and dreamer, too. He had thought about this before. Months ago he had come into Cimarron and stopped there briefly. No one knew him there, and he had loafed about town listening to gossip. He had even gone into the bank to change some money, and had glanced at the safe. Yes, it was tough, but not too tough. It could be done.

Of the four of them, only Brad would be known in town, so if necessary the others could ride in and be located about town before anything was suspected.

After a half-hour of talking about the town, the bank, the safe, everything—and then more time refining their thoughts, arguing about a few of the fine points, and settling into a plan, Brad got up. He had nothing more to say, so he went outside and stood at the end of the porch looking down the trail.

It was very hot. A dust devil danced in the distance, the sky was wide and empty, and the Wildhorse Park meadow stretched off toward Moreno Valley below. Far down the trail among the dancing heat waves he saw two riders. They seemed tall in the mirage made by the shimmering heat.

Those riders were Papa and me.

Brad told me later he felt a twinge of relief when he saw us coming. And anticipation. I must say that I did not feel the same way—not because I had not been thinking about him on the ride, but because I had no idea we would see him here. We were sure he had been heading to Cimarron. To see him this far south of town was a surprise.

Brad also told me later that he had been a little apprehensive about Papa. Brad had known him in those days before I did—or at least had heard about him. Only about half of what you hear on the trail is ever true, but what Brad had heard—that Papa had been a gunman for the big cattle outfits, and had killed eleven men—was enough to make him wary, despite Hondo's recommendation and the fact he was now riding with his daughter.

Brad went to the trough at the edge of the plaza and dipped up a bucket of water, then went back among the trees to strip down to his waist and bathe, dipping another bucket to complete the job. He discarded his old shirt, and went back to the store for another.

Papa and I were riding into the yard as he crossed to the store, and I could not help but notice his broad, powerfully muscled shoulders. He went into the store and pulled from the shelf a dark red shirt with bone buttons, and slipped it on. When he came out again, we were taking the horses to the corral.

"Where's Burns?" Papa asked.

"Gone to Cimarron."

Papa and I went inside, and after a moment Brad followed. Jeffcoat was balancing a knife in the palm of his hand, and as we entered he suddenly caught it by the tip and flipped it into the calendar across the room. It stuck there, and quivered. He was just showing off, but I will say that his ability with that knife made an impression.

Little did I know that in a few days that ability would save our lives.

Chapter 4

Wildhorse Park was high, over 9,000 feet in the sky. In the winter it could get bitterly cold and the wind would blow a gale for days at a time. Even in the summer it got cool at night, cool enough—occasionally—for frost.

But on this July day it was still and hot. Outside, a black-and-white magpie, what the Mexicans called a *urraca*, let out a cackle. A mockingbird sang in a cottonwood tree back of the store.

An empty buckboard came up the trail from Moreno Valley, flanked by two riders, but it stopped only long enough to water the horses. It was headed down to Rayado, and then beyond to Springer and the railroad depot, where it would load supplies and make a much slower ride back to Taos.

"Never figured you to have a family, Dave," said Hondo, glancing at me. "And she's no youngster, either."

"She's been to school in Texas," Papa said, and I could hear a touch of pride in his voice. "More than you and me can say."

"That's true enough," Hondo said. "Though I did learn to read along the way, and I always have a book with me, so I am not"—and here Hondo affected a somewhat comic and haughty tone—"insensitive to the benefits of education."

Papa laughed, and even Brad smiled. "Now I remember what I liked about you, Hondo," Papa said.

"Well, even though I never figured you for a family man, you got one now. Where are y'all headed and what are you planning to do?"

Papa told them of our plans for a California farm, or maybe something more—and about wanting to see this country one last time before heading west. Brad spoke up.

"The California part doesn't sound half bad. I've always wanted to see the Pacific Ocean." Brad paused for a moment, as if the idea took him to some place far away, and suddenly he remembered where. "You know," he said. "That was one of the things Will Kane used to say. He was all the time saying he wanted to see the ocean, which was funny coming from someone up here in the mountains...." Brad's voice trailed off. Then, he looked at Papa again and said, "But riding through this country for fun—well, I'm not sure you haven't already gone around the bend."

"We'll make it," Papa said. "Though we didn't plan on running into you boys. That changed our plans somewhat. I had figured on going into Cimarron, but after running into y'all up in the Valle Vidal, we stayed away. They might figure I was riding with you and I'd be on the run again, family or no family."

"Yeah. Well. Sorry about that."

Brad went outside again, and I had a sense, for the first time but far from the last, that he was sorry about a lot of things. I must admit that from those first days I was curious about him, even though he was ten years older than me—no, I may as well admit it now, more than ten years. But on this day, he just seemed quiet, stern, and sort of sad.

Papa leaned over and whispered to Hondo: "Is he as good as they say?"

Hondo nodded. "Better. He's as good as any I've ever heard of, Dave, and you know I've seen them all—Courtright, Allison, Hardin, Hickok, Stoudenmire, Pink Higgins. All of them. He's a planner. That's what makes him so good. And he keeps his emotions out of it."

"Well, it sure doesn't seem that way with Cimarron," Papa said.

Hondo nodded, letting that sink in. "Yeah. That's got me

worried a bit, too. It's personal with Cimarron. But so far everything has been by the Bradshaw book. Every step mapped out.
And he lets us tell him if we think something ain't right. Can you
imagine Clay Allison doing that? I've seen Allison pistol-whip a
man for questioning him."

"Even so. Y'all be careful," Papa warned. "I know Will Kane,
and he's no man to be trifled with."

"Bradshaw knows that. They used to ride together. They were
saddle partners."

Papa shrugged. "Well, that gives him some advantage, I guess.
But it also gives Kane an edge, too."

I got up and walked out on the porch. Brad stood alone near
the corral. One of the horses came up to him, perhaps expecting a treat, but all Brad did was absent-mindedly rub the horse's
nose. It was a look I would come to know well in the years—the
decades—ahead, but it was a mystery to me then: Brad working
out a plan in his head. He would be deep in thought, and then
his hands would move. He told me he was visualizing things,
talking them through. Once or twice, when he thought no one
was around, I caught him talking out loud. When I asked him
about it later, he had no idea he was doing it.

The monsoon season comes to northern New Mexico in July
or August. But this year was dry, and the monsoons were late.
The lack of water would be an asset for Brad and his men, who
knew the country. A meadow that looked dry might have a de-
pression in the middle that—if you dug down a few inches with
a bowie knife or even with a stout stick and your hands—would
start to seep water. And as they rode farther south toward Mexico
they would encounter the *tinajas*, the natural dips in the rocks
that would hold water for a few days. Not a lot of water, but the
difference between life and death in desert country.

Not that Brad expected the posse to follow them that long.
Once they hit the bank in Cimarron, they would ride hard on
borrowed horses for fifteen miles to Lookout Meadow, where
Burns would have their own horses stashed.

They could make the switch there. When the posse found the

borrowed horses, some of them would turn back, knowing they were now chasing a much smaller party on much fresher horses. The likelihood of catching them would go down considerably.

But Will Kane and a few men would ride on. And they would be tough men, hired guns from the mining company whose money they had taken. They would keep up the search because they had to…and they would want to. They would have their fur up, as Hondo would say. The chase would be on.

They would ride south through the mountains for a hundred miles. It would be rough going and on their fresh horses they would put yet more distance between them and their pursuers. Then Brad planned to do something Will Kane would not expect. He would turn east out of the mountains and on to the plains, and then head straight south to Mexico across the high plains and desert of eastern New Mexico. It was risky business—300 miles of nothing—but it was the fastest way to safety and that was the way they would take.

By then, the monsoon would surely have started, and the *tinajas* should contain just enough water for their horses and themselves. But the posse pursuing them would not be able to get by on such scarce offerings. They would give up the chase.

Still, the amount of money he hoped to get away with would mean the bank and the mining company and the ranchers would go to extraordinary means to keep them from Mexico. So they would cut telegraph lines as they went into town, and they would cut a few as they found them along the way—Jeffcoat could shinny up a telegraph pole faster than some people can walk across flat ground. But they couldn't cut them all. For one thing, they didn't want posses to follow their route by the cut lines. So despite this precaution, they had to figure that every town between Cimarron and Mexico would know they were on the loose within a day or two of the robbery.

I watched Brad by the corral, walking, smoking a cigarette, moving his hands as if he were explaining the plan to a child. Visualizing every step. It was a simple plan, really, but plenty could still go wrong. Once the word got out, every lawman and adventure seeker in New Mexico Territory would be after them. And not a few outlaws, who might decide that robbing Brad was easier than robbing banks. That was what concerned Brad the most: men who had no qualms about just shooting them on sight.

Brad had not shared one part of his plan with the gang, the part he was still working out in his mind, and that was when and how they would rob the bank itself. It didn't make sense to rob the bank in the middle of the night, as they had done in Raton. For one thing, after the Raton job, it's likely Cimarron would be on the lookout for that. So how do you hit Cimarron in a way they would least expect? In the middle of the day, in broad daylight. With the whole town watching.

The final pieces of Brad's plan would come when Rye Burns got back from Cimarron. Burns would come back with all the information he needed. Getting information was what Rye Burns excelled at, and Brad expected he would this time, too.

Will Kane's wife Sydney could not help but be a part of Brad's plan, and that part caused Brad some sadness, for Brad truly cared for Sydney—or, at a minimum, had nothing against her.

She had made the only wise choice available to her at the time, even though Brad had hated her for it. Of course, Brad would have said that he hated the world, and even himself then. But setting all that aside for now, she had chosen wisely, given her options. Will Kane had grabbed the brass ring. He had come in out of the cold. He had been given one of those chances in life which you don't get that often, that most of us don't get ever: to erase our past, to come out of the darkness and into the light.

Will Kane had grabbed that chance. And Brad Bradshaw knew that if he had been given that chance, he would have grabbed it too.

Sydney was a tall, pale girl. She was blonde—or was then. She was intelligent, so Brad and everyone who knew her said. Later I asked Brad if he had been in love with her. He said no, but I don't know if he said that for me, or because he now knew what real love meant and he found what he felt for Sydney was not it.

Love or not, his pride had certainly been hurt when she had jilted him for his friend. And it wasn't just that. Both Brad and Will were young men then, boys really, I can say now. They were doing what boys do: seeing how close to the edge they could get without tumbling into the abyss. And from Brad's point of view, Cimarron had reached out and grabbed Will and dragged him back from the abyss, while it gave Brad a good swift kick over the edge.

Folks say time is a healer, but it is not. Forgiveness is the healer. Time is a thief. It robs a man of his years. It robs him of his life. Only love and forgiveness truly heal.

That's why Brad wasn't just planning the robbery out by the corral that evening at Wildhorse Park. He was telling himself: "This will be my last ride in the night. My last run for the border. I will have that Mexican ranch. Or maybe, one day, when everyone has forgotten, perhaps I'll go to California. I should like to see the Pacific Ocean, too."

II

The wind skittered dust devils along the ground, and Brad looked up quickly and saw me. He smiled a sheepish smile as he knew I had caught him talking to himself, using his hands. He turned to the horses, checking their legs and their shoes.

The day turned to dusk. In the mountains of New Mexico, at least in the summer, there comes a moment in the early evening when the air, which is often oppressively hot during the day, with one cool breeze signals the coming of the night. Off to the west, across Moreno Valley in the mountains beyond, clouds had formed. An occasional flash of lightning brightened the darkening sky.

Rye Burns rode in hours later, long after the sun had dropped below the horizon. Brad walked out to meet him, and took the heavy sack from his hands. Rye swung down and turned his back to the horse, but the horse restlessly pushed against him.

"Some outlaws killed two men and burned a place out east, south of Springer, near Watrous headed toward Santa Fe." He glanced toward the store.

"They say who did it?" Brad asked.

"They say you did. Or, rather, they say the same outlaws who hit the Raton bank did it. 'Course, there's also folks saying Indians did it. There always are."

"Indians? Y'all haven't had Indian troubles around here in years have you?"

"No. Most of the Jicarilla Apaches were hauled off to the reservation, but there's a few who refused to go, and they still get blamed for just about everything. And truth be told, there are a few bad ones. There's a few bad apples in every barrel, I guess, whether that barrel's painted red, brown, or white. Anyway, hating the white man—or at least the white man's government— has become popular among Indians these days," Burns said.

"Can't say as I blame them much for that," Brad said.

Burns didn't argue that point. He just let it hang in the air for a beat before asking, "Who's inside?"

"Dave Stanton and his daughter."

"Stanton?" Burns looked at him quickly. "Is he with you?"

"He's quit. He's headed for California with the girl."

"This here is no time to travel with a woman."

"Well," Brad said. "You're talking to the wrong man about that." Then, "What'd you find out?"

"The mine has a payroll at the bank, all right. About thirty thousand. Probably about twice that in the safe, all told."

Thunder rolled, and a gust of wind whipped dust into a cloud. There was a brief spatter of rain, and both men started for the barn with Burns' horse. Having to take a minute to get out of the rain gave Brad a moment to compose himself. Sixty. Thousand. Dollars. It was far more than he had thought would be there in his wildest dreams.

"To go into town we'll need four horses that nobody knows."

"I got four in the upper pasture you can use," Burns said.

"We'll need for you to leave our own up at Lookout Meadow."

"I can do that."

"What else did you see?" Brad said.

Burns was stripping the saddle from his horse and placed it astride a sawhorse in the tack room. "I saw Kane. He looks fit."

No surprise. Will Kane was not the kind of man who would let himself go to seed. Will had always been ready for what might come his way. When they rode together, Brad would sometimes ask, "You ready?" whenever they would head out somewhere. Kane's answer was always the same: "I was born ready."

Brad once told me of a time when his horse lost its footing on a narrow mountain trail and started over the edge. Will Kane's rope had come out of nowhere and dropped around his waist just as he was going over. Brad was still in his stirrups and squeezed his horse tightly with his legs. It was just enough for the horse to find his footing and keep both of them from falling two hundred feet almost straight down and to a certain death. It had all happened in a flash.

Of course, Brad had saved Kane's life a time or two as well. It was nothing they talked about, except in joking, and it took me years to get the stories out of Brad. "All in a day's work," he would say.

The rain came suddenly, and it fell hard. The two men ran for the store and stopped on the porch, listening to the roar it made on the roof. It was a first-rate gully washer. Rain is usually welcome in this dry country, but this time it was not welcomed by Brad. It would complicate his plan, which depended at least in part on there being no water on their getaway trail.

Brad took a deep breath and took in the peculiar smell of parched earth when first touched by rain—somewhere between sweetness and a steely mustiness.

On the porch the two stood together in silence. Then, after a long minute, Burns said, "The money's there all right. No question about it. When I went into the bank, they were counting the gold into sacks."

"Hear anything else?"

Burns paused a split second. Was he trying to remember, or was he trying to decide whether to tell what he had heard?

"That job y'all pulled off a week ago...."

Brad stiffened up. How did Burns know that had been him? He quickly thought it through. The days that had passed, the fact that there had been four men—no mystery there. Even though they got away cleanly, the posse would have seen the tracks and eventually found the four abandoned horses. And then Brad shows up at Burns' place with Hondo and Jeffcoat and Romney. It would not have been so hard for Burns to connect those dots.

"The folks in Cimarron were talking about it."

No surprise there, either. In this country it was the kind of news that traveled fast. But did they know it was him? As far as anyone in Cimarron knew, wasn't Brad long gone from this country?

"Plenty of folks still remember the bad blood between you and Kane," Burns said, as if reading Brad's mind. "And a few of them are putting two and two together and coming up with the four of you headed back."

"You didn't say anything, did you?"

"Course not," Burns said emphatically. Brad instantly regretted asking the question. Burns was a man who kept secrets. For Brad to question that came dangerously close to an insult, and Brad did not want to insult the man on whom the success of this job—and perhaps even his life—depended.

"Course not," Brad repeated. "I didn't mean anything...."

"No offense taken," Burns said. "But you just need to know... They might be expecting you."

Chapter 5

It might have been any cow-country general store at that hour, with rain on the roof and Jeffcoat sitting at a table under a coal-oil lamp idly shuffling a pack of cards in his big brown hands. Hondo and Papa sat at one side on the counter, swapping stories of the old days.

Romney cornered Burns and Brad as the two men entered and went off in a corner, arguing with them.

They might have been any group of cowhands waiting for the rain to pass, but tomorrow there would be quick, careful movements, horses pushed to their limits, perhaps the roar of guns. Tomorrow they would ride into Cimarron.

Brad broke off with Romney and came over to where Jeffcoat was doing tricks with the cards. We all watched, fascinated at the flowing, smooth movements of Jeffcoat's brown hands. The man was a marvel with cards. An old scar on the Indian's face stood sharply clear under the lamp.

Papa turned to Burns. "I owe you for supper."

"That's all right. You're a friend of Hondo. Forget it. Besides, your little girl didn't eat that much."

I blushed, and Papa smiled. He knew Burns would be well-paid for helping Brad do this job. Burns took a package from the counter and handed it to me.

"What is that?" Papa demanded.

Burns shrugged his shoulders. "A present from Romney here."

Papa pursed his lips in that way he did when he was mad but not quite sure what to do about it. He ripped open the package, exposing several folds of cloth I had admired earlier. Abruptly he thrust the package back at Burns. He then turned on Romney.

"When my girl needs clothes, I'll buy them. She's not a stray you can throw a brand on."

"Take it easy, old man." Romney's tone was careless, and he underlined the "old man" with faint contempt.

Papa's face stiffened. "Why, you stupid little saddle pup."

Romney's hand dropped for his gun, but Hondo was too quick. He grabbed Romney, then stepped between them, stopping the half-drawn gun.

Romney wrenched at the hand, trying to tear free. But Papa had not just been watching. His gun had come smoothly and quickly into position, pointed straight at Romney's belly. In fact, if Hondo hadn't stepped in between, Romney would already be dead—and he knew it. He became suddenly very still. We all did. Romney looked past Hondo into Papa's icy gray eyes. The "old man" suddenly didn't seem so old. Romney was not a man given to fear, and even when he was afraid he was careful not to show it. But he knew death when he saw it. He had never seen a gun drawn so fast.

I do not know what got into me, but I was the first one to speak.

"He didn't mean any harm, Papa," I said. "He was just trying to be nice."

Everyone relaxed. Romney slid his gun back into his holster and held his hands to his side to show they were empty. Hondo loosened his grip and took a step back. Papa lowered his gun, too, though he had yet to holster it.

"Ali," Papa said. "I think it's time we turned in for the evening. These boys don't want an old man or a little girl around spoiling their fun. Why don't you head over to our room."

Papa gestured to the building across the plaza.

I was glad the light was low, because my face suddenly grew

very hot. I'm sure a part of it was fear, as I realized just how close that situation had come to violence. But I can now admit that a part of the rush of blood I felt was the excitement of knowing that I had been the cause of the little ruckus. Papa may have called me a "little girl," but every man in the room knew I wasn't one, including Papa.

And—from that moment on, I think—I knew it too.

I walked out of the door as Papa finally let his gun slide fully down into his holster. I paused on the front porch and heard Papa say, "Romney, if you're riding with Hondo I know you're not all bad, but do you remember what I told you about Ali a couple of days ago up in the Valle Vidal?"

"You said she was special to you."

"That's right. I did. And she is. And I'll thank you to remember it from now on."

"Yes, sir."

Papa walked out on the porch and put his arm around me. From inside the store we heard nothing for a few seconds. Romney stood silent. His anger evaporated into relief as he realized how close he had come to getting himself killed.

Then we heard him say, "Thanks. Thanks, Hondo."

"Forget it," Hondo said. "You had no idea, and I did." Hondo let out a little laugh. "You know, when we first saw him a few days ago, my first thought was that Stanton looked a whole lot older than I remembered. I wondered if he had lost his speed, but I sure didn't want to test him."

Hondo looked over at Romney. "I guess it's fair to say he hasn't."

Jeffcoat continued to shuffle the cards, the flutter of the deck the only sound in the stillness of the store. Hondo picked up his blankets and started across the plaza, and after a minute Romney followed.

I do not know for sure if they were tense, thinking about what they planned to do tomorrow, but I was nervous for them, and my nervousness—plus what had just happened in the bar—pretty much guaranteed that I was hours away from sleep. Papa and I shared a single, bare room. It had two cots made of planks, with a thin but comfortable-enough tick mattress on it—really nothing more than a canvas bag filled with straw–but after sleeping on the ground for the past week, it felt luxurious.

Even so, I was a bundle of nerves and energy. I rolled up in my blankets on my cot, but I lay awake, wide-eyed, thinking about the past hour. It was an hour in which my whole view of life changed—my view of Papa, of Brad, of men generally, and of myself.

I know there's perhaps more than a bit of romantic nonsense in what I'm about to say, and there's nothing I despise now more than romantic nonsense, but you must remember that I was sixteen then and still had—you might say—a tolerance, even an appetite, for romance and for nonsense. But I had begun to see Brad not as an outlaw, but as a man looking for a way out of the outlaw life.

I had certainly never met a man like him—not that I knew many men of any kind then. But even in my limited experience I could see he was different, the kind of man that other men would follow. Certainly Papa, despite his wariness, respected Brad, and Papa respected few men.

Papa, though, had long outgrown romanticism. That is, if you didn't count this very trip through the New Mexico high country, which was motivated by more than a dash of nostalgia. But even including this trip, it is fair to say that Papa was a man who saw through to the heart of the matter. On the ride down from the Valle Vidal to Wildhorse Park, he had said, "I'm not saying Brad and his men don't have a right to feel like they've been wronged. Life has dealt them a tough hand. But it's a fool thing that Bradshaw has in mind. They'll get themselves killed, and nothing more. Or worse, they'll get other people killed."

But can't people change? Papa had. He didn't talk about it much, at least not then—about his life before and what had suddenly caused him to send for me, and to try to make a new life for us in California. But one day up in Colorado City a man came up to us on the street and embraced Papa in a big hug. I was shocked. I had never seen Papa hug another person—at that point, he hadn't even hugged me. Papa introduced me to him as Father John Dyer. But Father Dyer said, "It's not because I'm a priest. I'm just old!" And he let out a big, infectious laugh. Turns out Father Dyer was a Methodist preacher.

Father Dyer asked me a few questions about myself, which I must have answered, though I was still in such shock about Papa being friends with a preacher that I don't remember what I said. All I remember was what Papa said, "I can never repay you, John. You saved my life."

Father Dyer put a big hand on each of Papa's shoulders and said, "It wasn't me, and you know that. And I should be the one thanking you, Dave. You helped this old preacher believe in God again."

I thought about all of this as I lay on my cot in the dark. The rain had brought an extra coolness to the night, but the room we were in, with the windows and doors closed off, had begun to get stuffy. Water dripped from the eaves outside. I was happy not to be sleeping on the ground, but this was no luxury hotel. My head filled with the smell of the damp canvas and the sweating adobe walls. The dry, clean bed of my boarding school days seemed long ago and far away, though in fact it had been just months.

During the years I had been in school, it hadn't seemed so strange that Papa was off in the West. All the girls there were away from their families. All of the girls had fathers who were traders, or businessmen, or ranchers—which is what I told everyone my father was, but which I never really quite believed even as I was telling the stories.

As I considered the stories I told, it came to me: We are all the same, really. Aren't we? Yes, Brad was a bank robber, Papa had been a hired gunman who I was beginning to realize had killed men. But I was a liar myself. We all had our secrets we wished we could keep hidden.

After enough turning and twisting, I finally sat up. Papa was asleep. I looked toward him in the darkness, suddenly feeling a great love for him, but also pity. He was a hard man, but when he pulled his gun on Romney this afternoon I guess I realized for the first time just what a different man he had become. Compared to the cold-blooded instinct and speed I saw, I would say that what I see most of the time now is tenderness by comparison.

Was Brad like that? Could he be gentle if given a chance, and a reason?

It was close in the tightly shut room, and I felt stifled. I rose with care. Even though Papa slept more soundly these days than before, I knew that the least noise would arouse him. I pulled on my clothes and quietly made my way toward the door. With one more glance toward Papa, I eased the door open and stepped out on the long veranda.

After the hot, stuffy room the rain was cool and pleasant. I crossed the yard toward the stable, liking the feel of the mud between my toes, like when I was a little girl.

I had not had a lot of truly happy days when I was a girl. After Mama died and Papa went away, a deep sadness—I know that now—fell over me. Mama's family took me in, and they were lovely people who treated me well. No, they treated me more than well. My mother was dead and my father was gone. I was essentially an orphan, and yet I lived a life few orphans had any reason to hope for. Certainly a much better life than Jeffcoat or Hondo.

Still, I always felt I was an obligation to Mama's family. They were generous people and never said or did anything to make me feel like I was a burden. But I could not shake the feeling. The world just seemed broken.

The few times I felt happy and free when I was a little girl were when I was with horses. I would go to them often. They never failed to nuzzle me. Perhaps they sensed my need to be nuzzled, I don't know. But horses—at least partially—satisfied my need for affection and tenderness.

A flash of lightning off to the west revealed the skyline of the high mountains on the other side of Moreno Valley. Thunderheads were all around, but there were also patches of clear sky, and the moon was out and would occasionally peek through as the clouds moved swiftly from west to east. The plaza would go from pitch-blackness to being bathed in light and then back to darkness in surreal flashes.

I walked to the barn and entered just as it started to rain again. The horses snorted gently at first, and then settled down. I could see the whites of their eyes in the dim light of the barn. I whispered to them and rubbed the neck of the mare.

The mare's head bobbed suddenly, and I turned swiftly to see Brad come through the curtain of rain and into the barn. I drew back against the stall's side, startled, and perhaps a bit frightened.

"You shouldn't be out here at this hour, Ali." He spoke quietly, and my fears left me.

"It was hot and stuffy in our room," I said. "I was just out for a breath of air."

"I know, but you can never tell what's out and about in this country at night. Bears. Bobcats, even panthers. Not to mention prowlers and outlaws."

I smiled. Yes, outlaws, I thought. Like the one standing before me. But I did not say that. In those days I had very little experience talking with men. In later years, my lady friends and even Brad would tell me I had "man skills." Brad would say, "You think like a man." Perhaps it was true. If it was, perhaps it was because of this very trip. I don't know.

But in those days I certainly did not have the words to say what was on my mind. I did not have the words to tell Brad of my loneliness, or of the attraction I felt for him even in these initial meetings. So Brad himself broke the ice.

"I shouldn't be talking with you," he said. "Your Papa would not be happy if he knew the two of us were out here alone, and I wouldn't blame him."

"Papa likes you," I said.

"I don't think so," Brad said.

Brad was right. "Well," I said, slowly. "Papa would like you under different circumstances." Then, after a second: "He respects you." Then, after another beat: "So do I."

I don't know why I said that, but when I did I could feel my face blush.

"Do you know what I do—who I am?"

"You're an outlaw," I answered. "But from where I sit, that doesn't make you a whole lot worse than a lot of men I know who are not outlaws."

Brad said nothing for a moment. Then: "You know, Ali, I used to tell myself that, too. And I guess there's some truth to it. I used to tell myself that doing bad things didn't make you a bad man. But being a bad man means you'll do bad things. And we're all bad men...and women...to one degree or another..."

Brad's voice trailed off. A minute passed in silence. Then more. We stood together, shoulder to shoulder, our arms touching as we leaned against the wall of the barn and looked out at the rain. The squall that had brought us the rain had passed us and headed off to the east, to the plains of New Mexico and Texas. I could still see an occasional flash, hear a mutter or grumble of thunder.

Cool air had pushed in behind the storm. I tried to suppress a shiver—unsuccessfully. Brad felt my movement.

"You're cold," he said. "You'd better go in."

But I did not move to go. Instead, I leaned in toward him. He reached out and put his arms around me. He just held me, and the warmth of his body caused my shivering to stop. After a minute, or two, or...I don't really know how long, I said, "After.... After this job. What will you do?"

"Go down to Mexico."

I knew about Mexico. Mexico was that place you went when there was no place left to go, when you were being chased by men who knew all your hiding places. It was not that you couldn't be found in Mexico. It was just that if they found you there, they couldn't do anything about it. It was an irony. Those who obeyed the laws could be free in a land of laws, but those who lived outside the law could be free only in a land with no law.

Mexico. Papa had told me that when he was a boy, men in trouble or who wanted to live outside the law went to Texas.

I never thought until this moment that this might be one of the reasons I was born there, that Papa had been in trouble, or wanted to live outside the law. But that had changed, both for Papa and for Texas.

"Will you ever come back?"

"Maybe." Then, after a few seconds. "I don't think so."

I heard something, and I knew Brad heard it too. We let go of each other and he turned around, grabbing a pitchfork that had been leaning against the wall. Suddenly a man stepped into the barn and faced them. It was Papa, and he had a gun in his hand.

He gestured toward me, and said, "Ali, get to the room."

"It's not what you think, Papa."

"You're jumping to conclusions," Brad said quietly. "There was nothing wrong. She came out to be with the horses, and I heard something and came to check. That's it."

I don't know how long Papa had been standing there before we heard him, but it had been long enough to know that what Brad was telling him was the truth. We were all on edge, and all of us had obviously had trouble sleeping. Papa lowered his gun and spoke gently.

"Well, none of us need to be spending any more time out here in this barn. We've all got plenty to stay alert for tomorrow."

"That's true enough," Brad said.

And with that we all quietly found our way back to our rooms. I wiped my muddy feet the best way I could with an old horse blanket, found my bedroll and sank down into it, wrapping my arms around myself as I remembered Brad's arms just recently around me, and I drifted off to sleep.

Chapter 6

Rye Burns' store was tucked in just far enough up the side of the mountains rising to the north that it had magnificent views in three directions. When we had arrived the evening before—essentially skirting around the eastern edges of Moreno Valley and then climbing up to Wildhorse Park from the west, I had not noticed that you could look out from the veranda and see a hundred miles to the east, maybe more.

With the hard ride the day before, and the late-night excitement with Brad and Papa, I did not rise early. Brad's gang left long before it was light, headed toward Cimarron. When I stepped out on the veranda, Papa sat in a straight-back chair with a cup of coffee in hand, watching the sun rise out of the plains.

We would see no sunrises like this in California, at least not where we were going. The spectacle was sunset, into the Pacific Ocean, not sunrise. It did not occur to me until many years later what that difference might explain—what it might mean when the high point of existence was the beginning of the day rather than the beginning of the night.

In any case, living in Colorado for nearly a year with Papa, I realized I had already learned to love the land I would now have to learn to live without. For a second, a bit of anger against Papa welled up in me, and it surprised me. Where had it come from? Was I angry that Papa was teaching me to love a land that we planned to leave forever, or at least for a very long time? Or something else.

There was last night, of course. I guess I was angry about the way he had treated me in front of Brad—like a child. But I could not stay mad at him for that. When I thought that through I came quickly to the realization that he was just being my father, perhaps for the first time. I loved him more for at least trying to be a father than I was angry that he wasn't getting it just right yet.

Still...maybe I was angry at him for all the years he wasn't around to be my father. I know Papa felt guilty about what he had done, and I told him and myself that I had forgiven him. But had I? I do not mean to excuse him, or let him off easy. He had abandoned me to the care of near-strangers. He had done bad things. Yes, he had been broken by the war, and by losing his wife, but other men had endured such things and more, and they had not run away. So let me say it again: I do not excuse him.

But he came back, and by doing so he asked forgiveness and began showing me his love in the best way he knew how. And so I forgave him, and I forgive him still.

I padded up to him in my bare feet. He cradled a tin cup of coffee in his hands, in his lap. He faced east toward the sunrise. I put my hand on his shoulder.

"It's beautiful, isn't it Papa?"

"It is."

We watched in silence until the sun turned from a soft orange ball into a fire that became too bright to look at.

"Burns's got coffee in the store, if you want any."

"I'll get some in a minute. I want to pack first."

In less than an hour we were on the trail.

In that remarkable way things work in the Southwest, yesterday's rain had almost immediately greened up the country. The needles of the ponderosa pines seemed to fatten up with water. The scrub oak leaves that had been turning brown almost immediately regained some of their color. Even so, we saw little or no standing water. What water the plants did not suck up—either by leaf or root—quickly got absorbed into the ground, or it evaporated.

I knew this would change Brad's plans somewhat—or at least cause him some anxiety if he stuck to the current plan. He had banked on the trail being hard and dry—at least for his pursuers. But this country had suddenly become an oasis, and in the high country of Wildhorse Park, the views west—toward the still snow-covered Taos Peak, and the spine of mountains reaching north and south—were spectacular.

"It's beautiful, Papa."

"It is that," he said. "This is no country to raise a family, but I wanted you to see it, Ali. And I could not leave this country without seeing it again myself. This…"—and he waved his right hand toward the west as if he were a master of ceremonies presenting to an audience—"this is what I wanted you to see. People can talk all they want about the Alps and the Andes, but this here is God's finest sculpturing, if you ask me."

I could not help but smile at this. Whatever anger I might have stored up disappeared as I looked out across the New Mexico landscape.

This morning the tracks of animals and birds were sharp on the unblemished trail, but we saw no tracks of horses nor of men, at least not right away. Still, Papa's cold eyes swung to the hills, searching for any sign we were being trailed or watched. Some folk—and not just Indians—still used smoke signals in this country, due to the heights and distances. But we saw none.

Until just a few years earlier, the Comanches and the Kiowas—Plains Indians—had raided the Jicarilla Apaches that lived in this country, driving them high into the mountains. All those wars had ended by now, though, and the Plains Indians, at least in this part of the country, had been subdued, and the Jicarilla Apache had come down out of the mountains and were in a poor and motley state. Those who had not been herded off to the reservation had taken the most menial of jobs, mostly in Cimarron, to hang on to a pitiful existence.

But a proud remnant of all three tribes, plus outlaw white men and a few Mexicans, sometimes roamed as gangs. And until just a few years ago the Colfax County War had raged in this part of the country, breeding lawlessness all around. Will Kane did not end the Colfax County War, but he was a big part of bringing peace to Cimarron. Some of the outlaws Will Kane had run out of Cimarron did leave the country. As I already said, the notorious Clay Allison went back to Texas, where he died a drunk after falling off a wagon.

But the Colfax County War had bred its share of outlaws who didn't leave, and bad men had a way of finding each other, of banding together and causing mischief, even murder—at least until they turned on each other, as they inevitably did.

So even in the midst of all this beauty, I could see that Papa was worried, and he kept an eye on the horizon. I know that was one of the reasons he had been brusque with me, and with Brad, the night before.

We rode on, but we both had the same things on our minds, so after nearly an hour of silence, it was no real surprise to me when Papa said, "There's good men around. I don't want my daughter marrying a gunfighter."

"My mother married one," I shot back.

That silenced him, as I knew it would. Mother had married him, and it had been the making of him. After his rough and wasted life, she had tamed him down without making him less a man. The few good years he had had in this life—up until then, anyway—had been not just with her, but because of her.

I also knew that Papa, in his own way, admired Brad. Any man to whom Hondo would run second was a man not without his finer qualities, shall we say. And Jeffcoat, too. Jeffcoat had always played a lone hand except for once, the one time he had been in with another outfit that tried to rob the Cimarron bank. Jeffcoat had been the only survivor of that raid, and it had been one of the reasons Brad had no trouble recruiting him for this escapade. Jeffcoat, Hondo, Brad—they all felt they had, in their own ways, been wronged, and turning outlaw was their way of getting even, of administering justice in a country where justice was a rigged game. Maybe that was why, from the first time we met up in the Valle Vidal, Brad did not seem like an outlaw.

Even so, an outlaw he was. And as we rode south out of Wild-horse Park toward Mora and the Pecos Mountains that stood between us and Santa Fe, I had little hope of ever seeing him again. It must be said, though, that it has always been with very little hope that I had lived my life. So I had come to believe that a little hope meant…hope.

The sun soon turned the day hot. Off to the west, to our right, white fluffy clouds were beginning to form. That was the pattern in this country this time of year. Mornings cool and crisp and sharp, with clouds and often violent storms in the afternoon— only to be clear again by nightfall. Would it be like this in California? It suddenly seemed strange to me that Papa and I had not talked much about what we would do when we got there. For me, it had been enough just to be with Papa, but now…. Had it been meeting Brad that suddenly caused me to want a plan, to have a dream that was not just Papa's, but also my own?

"Papa, what will we do when we get to California?"

"If it is not too late in the season, we will plant a crop, and I will look for work."

"What will I do?"

Papa did not immediately answer. Could it be that the question had surprised him?

"Well, you will help me, I guess. Then, at some point, I expect you will find a husband…."

The trail before us turned up again, back into the mountains. The grass and sage of Wildhorse Park gave way to first ponderosa pine, and then to fir and aspen. We were in the trees, but occasionally we would break out of the trees onto an outcropping, or a place where a rock slide left a scar in the forest, and we could see out for miles. It was like nothing I had ever experienced before: the coolness in the middle of the summer. Back in Ft. Worth it would be unbearably hot and dusty. Even Colorado City—within sight of the mountains, at the very foot of Pike's

Peak—was still on the edge of the plains, and the heat on summer afternoons could be oppressive.

But this…. We climbed so high that even in July we found snow fields that were knee deep. Papa called it "corn snow," meaning it had melted and re-frozen and was full of holes, but it was a marvel nonetheless.

Papa glanced around.

"Smoke."

I followed his finger. The smoke was rising straight and tall from a low ridge off to the west. He watched it break, then break again, three dirty white pillows hovering and spreading out in the sky. In seconds they were gone.

Turning in the saddle, he looked back. I turned to see where he was looking and I saw behind us more smoke off to the north. There were people behind us. Were they following us?

"We'll eat," he said suddenly. "We may not get a chance later."

Papa pointed to an outcropping of rocks ahead and up to the left of where we were. It looked to be a place high enough so we could see all around us. I noticed that Papa slid his Winchester from its scabbard and we rode on toward the rocks.

We kept wide of the rocks until we were past them. Papa had me wait in a protected spot in the trees. Then he swung sharply around and rode up into them. When Papa was sure no one was there, he motioned me to join him.

He helped me down, and though I didn't need any help, I let him. We pulled out some biscuits and some dried venison.

"It's not much," he said. "But it will see us through for a few hours, and maybe we can find something to shoot and have a proper meal this evening."

I didn't mind the Spartan meal. Somehow, seeing that smoke, and even knowing that we didn't have a lot of food, didn't bother me. In fact, I felt a flush of excitement. I know now that what I was feeling was foolish—that I didn't fully grasp the danger of the situation. But I grasped enough of the danger to feel that we were really on an adventure. I could see the worry in Papa's face, and that caused me a bit of disquiet, but only a bit.

"That's alright, Papa. When we get to California, we'll have all we want."

Papa told me later that when I said that, something in his heart shifted. He had always been a resolute man, a stubborn man who did not mind hard work. And after Mama and Father Dyer, he had become a gentler man, and a protector. I had seen that in him myself.

But he had never been a builder, a leader of men, a shaper of empire—if I may use such language. Brad, now, I could see that in him from the first time I saw him, but not Papa.

But on that day, on the trail in the Sangre de Cristo Mountains in New Mexico, south of Cimarron and north of Santa Fe, Papa said he changed yet again. He became a man with a family, someone who wanted to build a legacy and an inheritance. He told me he had first felt that way about Mama, back in Ft. Worth, but her death had caused him to go a bit crazy. If his times with Father Dyer were his first steps back, this moment was the last step of his way back, and though to the eyes of Brad and Hondo and Romney and Jeffcoat he was an old man, he prayed to God he was not too old, that it was not too late.

II

We found a few sticks of dried-out wood fallen from a dead cedar up on the hill, and a few partly burned sticks left by some previous traveler. In a hollow among the rocks, where we could observe all who approached without being seen ourselves, I built a small fire for coffee. The wood was completely dry and made no smoke, only a faint shimmer of heat in the air.

As I worked on the fire and the coffee, Papa attended to the horses. He ran his hands over them to check for any abnormality, and checked their hooves.

My thoughts returned to Brad. Papa had known about Brad for a while. The grapevine of the trail, and saloon conversations, had given Papa a picture of this man who everyone said robbed banks, but whom no one had ever caught or even seen doing it.

I had come to find out there were three kinds of outlaws.

There were the kind that the newspapers wrote about. The Earps, Hickok, Billy the Kid, Clay Allison, and the like. "Do not envy these men," Papa would tell me.

In some ways I came to think of them like the Hollywood stars I would know later in life, in California. There is nothing glamorous about their lives. If they hate the attention as they should, their lives are miserable. And if they crave the attention, they have something broken inside them, and they find out soon enough that the attention does not satisfy the craving or fix the brokenness. Even more than that, all the attention keeps them from engaging in the quiet and sometimes lonely disciplines that would heal the brokenness.

Of course, there are other outlaws on the trail, men like Johnny Bull, Joe Phy, Luke Short, Longhair Jim Courtright, Jeff Milton, Dallas Stoudenmire, King Fisher, and Ben Thompson. Well known on the trail, but not to the public at large. But these men, too, led mostly miserable lives. They were, like Cain of the Bible, doomed to wander to and fro in the world. The difference is that Cain bore a mark to keep men from killing him. These men were marked in different ways. A reward on their heads made any man with a gun a potential enemy—and in this country that meant all men. Such men met one of two ends: they died with a gun in their hand, or in prison—often by the gallows.

Brad was, in a way, lucky—or perhaps he had planned it this way. People knew what he had done, but not who he was.

But redemption was possible. Papa himself was proof of that. And even Will Kane, in his way. He had been an outlaw, and he was now an officer of the law and a respected citizen. Western people are quick to forgive. They forgive anything but lies or cowardice.

A chipmunk moved closer, drawn by the smell of the venison perhaps. Papa called them "mini-bears" because they were as voracious as bears. I broke off a corner of a biscuit and tossed it to him. The mini-bear jumped away, but curiosity and the smell drew him back. He grabbed the crumb and ran off a few feet, turned to face me, and ate it.

The pause was brief. We quickly moved on, and the sun was hot. Magpies—large black-and-white birds with long tails—would occasionally caw. We passed through stands of aspen and the breeze would shake the leaves and branches into a background rustle. Once a rattler sounded off from the shade of a rock as we rode by. Above, a lone buzzard circled lazily against the clouds starting to billow up above us.

Papa must have also been thinking about Brad and his gang. When we stopped on an outcropping with a view back to the north, toward Cimarron, he said aloud: "Good luck, boys."

"Papa," I said. "Do you think they'll make it?"

He considered that question carefully. He considered the town of Cimarron and he considered Brad Bradshaw. After a while he commented, "He'll do it if anybody can." He paused briefly. "The trouble is, Ali, that's only the beginning. After that they chase you, and you run—if you're smart. Maybe you get away that time, but you can't always get away. When a man lifts his hand outside the law, he sets every man's hand against him.

"And you don't make anything. Leaving honesty out of it, you just can't make it that way. Mighty few outlaws ever sit down to figure out how little they make over the years.

"I knew a big time outlaw once—a man everybody talked about as being smart. That man spent a third of his adult life in prison, and had two death sentences hanging over him. By the time they did get around to hanging him he was almost too sick to stand up straight so they could put the noose around his neck."

Papa turned his eyes away from Cimarron, which we could not see anyway, it was now so far off to the north, and we headed south. We could see the plains of eastern New Mexico and Texas beyond off to the left, but they were in the haze near the horizon. Papa's eyes were focused on something closer at hand—along a ridge leading up to Ocate Peak, the tallest peak in this part of the Sangre de Cristos. I studied Papa's craggy face until his eyes narrowed, and I looked out, too.

Due east of us, another smoke was rising.

Chapter 7

While we were climbing through the high country headed toward Santa Fe, Brad and his men came to the outskirts of Cimarron. From Wildhorse Park they had ridden briskly to the east, toward Rayado, on the edge of the plains. Kit Carson had established Rayado thirty years earlier—in the 1850s—as an outpost against Indian raids on the settlers in the region, but it was now just a sleepy village with no more than forty or fifty folks scattered around a ford where the old Santa Fe Trail crossed the Rayado River.

Brad and his men rode in a wide circle around the village and kept going north toward Cimarron. They made a camp along the Cimarron River west of town. They built no fire that night, but they had plenty of grass and water for the horses they borrowed from Rye Burns. Brad wanted the horses fresh the next day. It would be a long, mostly uphill push designed to take the starch out of the posse that would be chasing them.

The next morning they kept circling and stood on the same bluff overlooking the town they had stood on just a few days earlier. They were right on the edge of Manley Chase's ranch. It was a beautiful spot, with the back side of the Tooth of Time—a landmark on the old Santa Fe Trail—straight ahead.

They went over the plan once again.

"You boys ride down this draw here and come into town

at twenty minutes to noon. Nobody knows you, so just ride straight in. You're just cowboys riding through. Get yourselves into place," Brad said, pointing to the bank.

"I'll be on the other side of town, by the corral and the blacksmith shop. There'll be some men and boys gathered round, likely. When folks start getting a whiff of trouble, the men will send the boys to safety, but they'll go get their friends and their mamas and pretty soon the whole town will be there."

Hondo smiled as Brad rehearsed every detail out loud. This is why he was fine riding number two. Brad had thought of everything.

"Once I get a crowd up, I'll start the fight. As close to noon as I can. I can promise you ten minutes...maybe fifteen, but no more."

Romney shook his head. "A hot day like this? That's a pretty long fight, even for you. What if he lands a lucky punch—or you do? It'll be over in a minute."

"I'm not trying to win," Brad said. "I won't be throwing many punches. I'll wrestle him if he'll let me. I'll keep my fists up and my chin down if he won't."

"That's still a long fight."

Hondo spoke up. "No matter. We won't need fifteen minutes. We'll be in and out in ten."

Brad eased himself in the saddle, looking down on the other three, and then past them toward the town.

"And no shooting. Even if they start shooting, no shooting back. If we get cornered in a gunfight, we're dead anyway. We can outrun 'em, but we are not going to out-shoot them. There's too many of them, and they will never stop hunting us down if we kill somebody's brother or daddy."

He started off, looking back once and saw them wave, and it gave him pause to realize what he was leading them into. They were good men—that is if you don't take into account the fact they were bank robbers. Good men or not, they were certainly tough. It suddenly seemed unlikely to Brad that they would all survive. Brad would tell me later that he did not believe in intuition or premonitions. He looked at the facts, and he calculated odds. "You don't make money if you don't take risks," he would say. "But I want a better than even chance of winning, and the more you put on the line, the better the chances need to be."

Brad told me many years later that he never expected to survive this robbery. When I asked him why he did it, he said, "Because I had come to hate my life. If this robbery could buy me a new life, it was worth doing, and if I died trying, that was okay, too."

But it would be many years before Brad had that clarity. All he knew as he rode across the ridgetop to put some distance between him and the boys was that if he survived, he would take his share of the money and he wasn't headed to Mexico. He would head to California and find me.

It was a strange thought to have just then, though, considering that he was headed to the home of a woman he once thought he loved.

II

Until a few days ago, Brad had a fixed map of Cimarron in his mind. It was a map of the Cimarron he had fled a half-dozen years ago to dive head-first into the outlaw's life.

But that map had failed him when he saw the town again a few days earlier. The town had changed. It had grown. A road came in from the northeast. It had been the old Santa Fe Trail, but now it was a well-traveled wagon road to Raton. If they had not been running from the law, it was the road they would have taken. You knew you were coming into Cimarron when you crossed Ponil Creek, which flowed south out of the Valle Vidal and emptied into the Cimarron River just outside of town.

Brad could not see the creek, but he could see the line of cottonwood trees that grew along it, off to the east of where he now stood. During most years the Cimarron River flowed strongly through town, and it was the river that caused the town to come into existence. The original Santa Fe Trail cut across the plains from Ft. Dodge, Kansas, to Santa Fe in an almost straight line.

It was the shortest way, and the fastest—if you survived it. But between the long dry stretches and the Indians, many a traveler chose the Mountain Route, which continued west from Ft. Dodge to Bent's Fort in Colorado. Then south over Raton Pass, through Cimarron and on south. The Mountain Route joined the main trail near Glorietta Pass, just thirty miles short of Santa Fe. It was longer, but wetter and safer.

Where the Santa Fe Trail crossed the Cimarron River, it became the main street through town. When Brad had last seen the town, there were only a few cross streets on the far side of the river from where he looked down on the town. No more than a couple of dozen buildings in all. The bank was where it had always been, on the main street, one block back from the river. The corral at the livery stable was on the outskirts of town to the east—also where it had been.

But almost nothing else was the same. The livery barn and blacksmith shop were larger than he remembered, with a dozen horses milling in the corral, and three large wagons that he could see. He knew there was probably at least one more wagon in the barn itself, getting worked on by the blacksmith, and likely a few horses in the stables, too. A thriving operation.

The rest of the town was bustling, too. The two or three cross streets he had remembered were now a dozen, or more. Brad spotted at least two buildings that looked like hotels—in addition to the St. James, which had been there when he used to come to town. The Cimarron River flowed west to east, and along the river for a mile or more in both directions were homesteads, some of them with irrigation ditches that brought water hundreds of yards from the river into catch basins or small ponds. The couple dozen buildings he had remembered had multiplied into a hundred or more—homes, businesses, outbuildings, barns, and sheds. This was not what he was expecting. But it was too late to turn back now.

He started to see a flaw in his plan. He had been banking on the fact that when he rode into town, folks would know there was about to be a fight. People would get excited, get ready for it. So the first thing he had planned to do was to make Will Kane good and mad. That would not be easy, for Will was a cool-headed man who thought things out carefully.

But if he could find Sydney, and perhaps make her feel a bit—well, a bit what? A bit scared? Yes, he did need to frighten her a bit, though he hated that. He had once cared for Sydney and the thought of frightening her was the one part of this plan that he found distasteful.

But he knew the one thing that would draw Will Kane into a fight would be to threaten Sydney, even if the threat was subtle and didn't put her in any real danger. So that was what he resolved to do.

A crowd would gather fast once the word of the fight got around. The fight would draw everybody down near the corrals, and probably only one man would be left in the bank. The holdup would be a smooth, fast job, no more than five minutes—it would have to be. With luck, it would be over and the boys would be away before the fight was over.

But Brad had developed his plan for the town he had left behind, not the town now before him. It was hard to imagine anything short of someone ringing the church bell in the middle of the night that could muster the entire town.

And what if something happened and guns were fired? Folks might interrupt their business for a few minutes to see a good fist fight, but no one would think it was a good idea to stick around and become the final resting place for a stray bullet. The crowd would scatter fast, and Brad would have to get out of town the best way he could.

And what if the boys had not yet robbed the bank? Would he leave them to face the town on their own? To save their own skins, would they give him up? Would they come clean and tell them that they had been the gang that had robbed the bank in Raton, and a half-dozen other banks in Wyoming, Colorado, and Kansas?

And what about Will Kane himself? What if he wouldn't be drawn into a fight? What if he grew suspicious and put two and two together? The first thing he would do would be to run to the bank, guns in both hands, deputizing any and all he ran into along the way and ordering them to follow.

Brad started his horse again. He drew his gun and spun the cylinder, then checked the spare gun he always carried in his saddlebag.

The horse he was riding was strange to him, but Rye Burns said it was the fastest he had. Their own horses would be waiting for them up at Lookout Meadow, which was not just a good spot for the switch—it was the perfect spot. It was nearly twenty miles away, and mostly uphill. Cimarron was at about 6,000 feet along the edge of the high plains. Lookout Meadow was over 9,000 feet in elevation, and the last couple of miles were especially rugged.

Brad had no doubt the posse would start following them right away, but even if the posse stayed on their trail all that afternoon, they wouldn't arrive at Lookout Meadow until sunset, see they had switched to fresh horses, and had continued on through some of the most rugged country in Colfax County. Some of the men would turn back there, and the rest would not want to follow after dark for fear of losing the trail. Brad and his men could ride on fresh horses through the night. Even at a slower pace in the dark, they would still put more miles between themselves and the posse by dawn.

The great difficulty, of course, came from what you couldn't plan for. The unexpected, the mistakes made by others which you can't foresee. A man packing a gun might walk into the bank at the wrong time. Somebody with a rifle handy might just happen to glance out a second-floor window and take an easy shot.

Or Kane might score a lucky punch and knock him cold. Just as bad, Brad might knock Kane out. The fight must last ten minutes at the very least. But just getting Will to the corral for the fight would not be a trivial problem to solve. Brad told himself he had thought of everything, but you never think of everything. So there it was again: "When you go to rob a bank, there's a thousand things that can go wrong, and any one of them can lead to the gallows, and if you think of half of them you're a genius."

The town was full of family men, but they were also dangerous men—and a few women. Take old Manley Chase's daughter Gretchen. She had married and left her daddy's ranch, but when her husband died she put on pants herself and roped and branded and always had a rifle or shotgun near at hand. And she had used them both to terrible effect at different times.

Brad tilted his hat back so his face could be plainly seen. When he heeled up on the edge of town he stopped. His mouth felt dry. He pulled on the stopper of his water bag and took a long drink. Then he tried to tamp down the butterflies in his stomach with the familiar routine of rolling a cigarette. Straightening himself in the saddle, he rode around the end of the corral and into the street.

Brad would say years later that being a movie producer was a lot like robbing a bank. You had to see the whole picture in your mind from the very beginning. You hoped nobody got hurt. And if you were very, very lucky you would get rich, though most of the time you just hoped to make enough money to try it again and maybe get rich the next time.

But producing movies was far in the future on the day Brad rode into Cimarron. What was not in the future was his ability to see the entire picture. In his mind he saw the whole town as though he soared above it. And not just Cimarron, but far beyond. Here lay the town. To the south he could see me and Papa riding through that part of the Sangre de Cristos they called the Pecos Mountains. Behind him, riding quietly into town, were Romney, Hondo, and Jeffcoat. He could see his escape route to the south, and then—after passing the Tooth of Time—he would turn west, up into the mountains. After changing horses they would continue heading south and west, out of the mountains and back toward the plains again, then dead south toward Mexico—300 hard miles with every gunfighter in New Mexico looking for them by then.

But it was also 300 lonely miles. Where they were going few

would want to follow—few would be able to follow. It would be an endurance race, and Brad and his men would be riding for their lives, while those chasing them would be riding only for a bit of reward money.

So it was a good plan. It was a plan that could work. But every step had to go just right, so Brad put everything out of his mind except the next step. Each step a small part of a machine he had already started in motion, moving inexorably toward a fixed point in time, a point in time that found him—finally—free.

The whole town knew Brad, or at least knew of him, but he was not a wanted man in Cimarron. Everyone suspected him of robbing trains back in Texas, and some in Cimarron still remembered the cattle he had caught and sold up in the Valle Vidal—but Will Kane had been his partner in those capers, and all of that was forgiven, or at least conveniently forgotten, now that Will was sheriff.

The town was still buzzing with news of the Raton bank, but no one had so far connected that to Brad. The bottom line: he could ride freely into the town.

Waves of excitement and anxiety and nostalgia crashed over Brad in quick succession. He had lived in Cimarron. He knew these people—or had known the folks who lived here then. And a few of them he had even liked. Will Kane had been the best friend of his youth. How many camp fires had they stared into together? How many close scrapes had they gotten each other out of? Too many to count. Too many, even, to remember.

And there was one woman in Cimarron he had not just liked, but loved, or at least thought he did—and in the next hour he would have to hurt her in a way that made him very nearly sick to his stomach.

But he quickly pushed that thought out of his mind, for he was—as he was fond of saying years later—"over the waterfall." The plan was in motion. There was no way back. The only thing left was to splash down into the water below, or onto the rocks, and keep moving.

Yes, keep moving. That was the essential part. Because even if he successfully robbed their bank they would pursue him as far as they could. They would capture or kill him if possible. Some of them might secretly admire him for pulling off such a hard job. And a very few of them—those who knew what the town had done to Brad—might even be glad that Brad had robbed the bank. Losing the money was the town's penance, its absolution, its offering—and Brad's recompense. They would not say that right away, at least not out loud, but in later years they would tell stories about him, maybe even sing songs about him.

But that would be years later. This year, if they could, they would hunt him down and shoot him like a mad dog that had gotten too close to the house.

So, yes, Brad Bradshaw knew these people. But what he knew about them—and himself—was changing. Some of the folks in Cimarron had been born here, of course. This was all they knew. But most of the people here—everywhere in the West— had come from someplace else. They were seeking something, or fleeing something—just like Brad was. They stood on one side of the law, and he stood on the other, but they were not so different.

Now though…. He could see that was changing. He had sensed it as he looked down on Cimarron from that last ridge before entering town, but he knew it then for sure. So many new buildings. So many new people he did not know. More people no longer seeking, or fleeing—but building. Building a life. A home.

And suddenly he knew this too: this would be his last job. His last robbery. He would either be caught, or killed, or he would take whatever he made off with—be it large or small—and that would be his grubstake. He would have to go to Mexico first, but after that…? Brad told me later that even that afternoon the dream of following me to California had popped into his mind. But the planner in him, the rationalist, the man who would become a builder himself—that man knew what a far-fetched notion it was.

Whatever. He might go to California or he might not. He

might head back east, or maybe just stay in Mexico. At this point he didn't really care. He would find a town where no one knew his name and he would become an honest man, if they would let him.

Brad rode through the main street of Cimarron. A couple of men who looked to be Jicarilla Apache sat on the long porch in front of the Maxwell Land Company's general store, which was two blocks down the street from the St. James Hotel, where Will had been plucked away from his outlaw life now nearly a decade ago.

Maria Vargas was sweeping off her steps.

A hen pecked at something in the street; a dog rolled in the warm dust. Several horses were hitched to the rail. One by one he checked off the things he saw, glancing once, sharply, at the bank from under his hat brim. Then he tilted it back on his head once more so people could see his face. He wanted to be recognized. His plan rested on everyone knowing he was in town.

As he drew abreast of the harness shop he saw a man who was standing inside come suddenly to the door and stare at him. He heard the startled exclamation: "Doc! Did you see what I just saw?"

Somewhere a door slammed. Brad Bradshaw had come back to Cimarron.

Chapter 8

B rad's first stop was Will Kane's house. From Rye Burns he knew where to find it. From where he had entered town, on the north side, he crossed the wooden bridge over the Cimarron River. The St. James Hotel was on his left. He turned left on a side road between the river and the hotel, and he saw Will's house in front of him. A coyote fence on the windward west side, a low adobe wall facing the street along the entire length of the home's city lot. The grass inside the wall was a rich, deep green, and the yard included some rose bushes and even a cherry tree. Brad smiled. Clever Will, he thought. He had used some old pipe to irrigate the yard by diverting water from the river. Will and Sydney had created a little oasis on this western edge of the high plains.

Across the road from Will Kane's home a big man with a luxurious black beard hollered out: "Hey, Brad! It's been a long time."

"It has been," Brad said, drawing rein. "Just passing through the territory and thought I'd call on some old friends."

"We never figured to see you around here again."

Brad dropped his cigarette into the street. Had he seen a curtain move in the Kane window? He grinned. "Why not? It's a free country, or at least it was the last time I checked. Besides, I wanted to see Will Kane. I hear he's been keeping in shape."

Brad glanced at the sun. Time was passing, and everything depended on timing, down to the minute, or nearly so. Brad came to a break in the adobe wall, a gate, directly in front of the house. He dismounted there.

This moment was, Brad told me later, the hardest part of the job for him, the most distasteful part. The plan was simple. He knew Will Kane would not be home in the middle of the day, and he knew Sydney would be. He had made sure that enough people in town knew he was there and the word would spread that he had walked in on Sydney alone.

His goal, in other words, was to make Will Kane mad enough to fight him, and nothing would do that like walking into a man's home unannounced and uninvited, and frightening his wife. Knowing Will as he did, Brad had no doubt the plan would work, but that didn't make it any less unpleasant.

Brad took off his hat and wiped his forehead with his bare hand. Even in the dry New Mexico heat, sweat had beaded up on his brow. His hair was wet with sweat. Or was it nerves?

He opened the gate and walked through. It had begun. He was not just walking on Will Kane's property. With that one step it became impossible to call the whole thing off—not that Brad wanted to.

For one thing, he wanted to see Sydney again. This house was her house, he could tell that right away. The neat porch. The painted boards and window sills. It was well cared for by a woman who cared. Will Kane just lived in it. That's what Brad used to say about all our houses, too. "A man's home is not his castle," he would say. "It's the woman's castle. The only interest the man has in it is paying for it."

No, a man also protects it, and Brad was counting on Will taking that interest seriously.

As neat and pretty as the house was, and as tense as Brad was, he also felt a sense of relief—a sense of relief that this was not his home, his life. Did he feel that way because he had met me? He would tell me that was a part of it. In any case, Brad said for the first time since Sydney had thrown him over for Will Kane, Brad felt no envy, no jealousy, no sense of being wronged by Will or the town. No sense that "all this could have been mine." He began to think that maybe she was not "the one who got away," but that he—in fact—was the one who had made a narrow escape.

He went up on the porch, his spurs jangling. There was a screen door, and the inner door was open. He stepped inside. It was an audacious thing to do. All these years later, I can scarcely believe he did it—to walk into a man's house unannounced.

Brad felt immediately out of place. This was not the cabin of a cow camp, with functional wooden furniture. This was a town home. A woman's home. There was a carpet covering the wood plank floor. There were winged chairs, and a couch. A couch! And it was covered in a plush fabric with white linens pinned carefully on the arms. It was a proud, pretentious little room, stiffly, primly...respectable.

The room was Sydney, so completely Sydney, that Brad for an instant felt sorry for Will. How much had she changed him?

"Anybody home?"

His voice boomed into the stillness within the house, somehow faintly indecent in that strict, upright stillness. Sydney Kane came suddenly into the room, and stopped abruptly.

I did not meet Sydney until many years later. We were both old women then, not as old as I am now, but too old for me to see her as she stood before Brad that day. I never quite trusted Brad's description of her on that day.

"She was shapely," he said.

"What does that mean?" I asked. I wanted him to admit that she was pretty, but he would not.

"It means she was not fat."

He did tell me she wore a neat house dress, with a bib apron over it. She had pulled her hair back in a ponytail to do the day's housework.

And Brad did add this: "She looked older."

"Older as if she was getting old before her time?"

"No, I mean older as if she had become a woman."

She had a certain assurance and poise he did not remember.

Was it just that they were kids then and grown adults now? Or was there more to it than that? When I was young and beautiful, men would stop their talking and turn their heads toward me. Today, I am an old woman, but I can still command a room—in a different way. I traded my beauty for power. Not in the way most people think, perhaps even in the way you are thinking. I came to learn that men would give beautiful women an extra bit of attention, so I resolved that when I got that extra bit of attention, I would make sure they saw something other than my beauty. As my beauty faded, what they saw in me remained.

It was a good trade. I was not going to be able to hold on to my beauty anyway, so why not trade it for something that would last? In her small world, in the best ways she knew how, perhaps this young woman was doing the same.

"Hello, Sydney."

Her face turned white to the lips, and she smoothed her dress with both hands, running them down over her waist, carefully, slowly. It was a gesture she used when she was upset. He remembered it well.

Sydney had always been…well, respectable. Brad walking into her home unannounced could not have been a more direct affront to that respectability. So when they came face-to-face in the drawing room of Will and Sydney Kane's home, Brad sensed instantly the outrage, but there was something more. A curiosity.

"I got a sense," Brad told me later, "that if I had just knocked on the door and stood there with my hat in my hand she might have invited me in and had been glad to see me, that we might have sat and talked and had a cup of coffee together."

But on this day that could not be.

Whatever desire Brad saw flash on Sydney's face—to just sit and talk, to let bygones be bygones—was replaced by the anger and fear she felt at seeing a man she believed to be an outlaw walking insolently into her home.

"What do you want?" she said sharply.

It was the reaction he wanted. No, not the reaction he wanted, but the reaction he needed. Brad was a threat, a danger. Yes,

I am, he wanted her to believe. So while it was the reaction he needed in this moment, it nonetheless made him simultaneously sad and angry.

"Where's Will?"

"He's not here." She gathered her apron in her fingers and seemed to dry her already dry hands. "What are you doing here? Why couldn't you stay away?"

"Figured we might talk over old times, Sydney." He grinned at her, a taunting grin. She flushed and grew angry.

"Go away. Go away and leave us alone."

Brad did not move. His eyes went to the clock on the mantel. 11:50. "I won't be staying," he said. "I just came back to see Will."

"You will see him if you stay. He isn't afraid of you."

Brad told me later that it was when she said that that he was truly ashamed for what he was doing. But all he did to show his shame was to lower his eyes to the floor and say softly, "Will? Afraid of me? No, Will was never afraid. It wasn't fear that..."

Brad looked up at Sydney. "It wasn't fear, at least not fear of me, that drove Will and me apart, that caused Will to come into town for an evening that put us on different paths, on this collision."

Sydney took a step back. What was Brad talking about?

"Was it love? Or maybe it was fear. Not so much fear of dying, but dying for no reason, with nothing to show for it. Is that what fear of God is?"

Sydney stared at him with her mouth open. Brad seemed to be having a conversation with himself, not with Sydney. He was. He was saying out loud the conversation he had been having with himself for the past day.

He glanced around the room and smiled. He could see that Sydney had no idea what he was talking about. Brad himself had no idea why he said what he said out loud, but in a strange way it served his purposes. It scared Sydney, and—seeing that—Brad remembered why he was there.

"Well, you must really have him hog-tied or he'd never sit

still for a room like this, Sydney." He looked into her eyes. "Better give him some rope, Sydney. You tie a man too tight and he strangles. You let a man have a little leeway, and if he loves you he will tie himself, and like it."

"Will isn't tied down," she protested. "He's a responsible man. He means something to this town."

She lifted her eyes to his again. "What do you mean to anybody? Anywhere?"

He felt the stab of truth, but brushed it away. Yet it was true, for he meant nothing, anywhere, to anybody.

But he thought of me, and he said, "You're wrong, Sydney. I've got a girl of my own." He knew it was not a fact. It was a hope. But in that moment it was enough.

Sydney was not buying it. "So what do you think she would say about you walking in on another woman, alone? Is this your idea of what a real man does when he has a girl of his own?"

"What does a real man do, Sydney? Pin on a sheriff's star, like Will did, so he could run his best friend out of town? Is that what a real man does? Betray his best friend?"

Sydney fired back, "You know Will didn't want to do that. He had to...after all that happened."

Brad's eyes flashed. "Is that what you and Will tell yourselves? That you had no choice? That you're sorry you had to throw me to the wolves, but there was no helping it?"

Sydney Kane was furious now. "You made your choices, Brad. Yeah, life may have dealt you a tough hand. Dealt Will a tough hand, too. This is tough country, you should know that better than most. Nobody hands you chances here. You make your chances, and you had plenty of good chances. You just didn't take them. Will did, and we have a life now." Her voice lowered to a hissing whisper: "So just get out. Get out of my house, and I hope I never see you again."

Brad wanted—with every fiber in his body—to answer back. But he didn't. Instead, he did just what Sydney asked. He turned on his heel and walked out, and stood there for a moment in the bright sunshine. Had that little tete-a-tete accomplished its goal?

Would walking into the house unannounced, unwelcome, make Will mad enough to fight?

II

The table was set. Brad's plan was so far unfolding just as he hoped. Even so, he felt uneasy. The uneasiness was not because he suddenly lacked confidence in his plan, but because he suddenly had lost his heart for it. He did not want to frighten Sydney. He would have loved nothing more than to have sat in one of those plush chairs in her overwrought parlor and drink coffee until Will Kane came home, and then—upon seeing him—to embrace his old saddle partner with slaps on the back.

How many head of cattle had they branded together? How many times had they fought off wolves or rustlers? How many calves had they pulled out of bogs or thickets? How many sunrises had they greeted together? How many spectacular sunsets had they silently watched?

He gathered his reins and stepped into the saddle, and suddenly Sydney was beside him, grasping at the reins in his hands, as if to keep him from wheeling around and riding off to confront Will.

"Brad...I don't care what you think of me, but don't hurt Will!" She clung to his hand. At the touch of her hand, Brad felt a flash of warmth go through him.

Sydney looked at him with anguish in her eyes. "Please, leave him alone. He won't tell you this, but he loves you. He hates what happened to you. We both do. I know this doesn't mean anything to you, Brad, but we pray for you. We pray you'll find peace."

The words seemed to embarrass Sydney. She lowered her head and took a step back. Then she looked up at Brad and said, "He won't draw a gun on you. He would let you kill him first. I'm telling you this because I don't think you know that. I'm telling you so you'll know there's no need to draw on him."

The words stopped Brad cold. He looked down at her round, clear face, now stained with tears.

A great tenderness welled up in Brad. The town had wronged him, and it had used Will Kane to do it. The town had given Will respectability, only it wasn't a gift. It came with a price, and that price was turning on his friend and running him out of town. Suddenly, though, Brad didn't care. He hated himself for frightening Sydney, and he did not want to fight Will.

But things were in motion. He knew that at this instant Hondo and Romney and Jeffcoat were waiting for the bank to clear so they could enter.

He said gently, "Sydney, you and I both know what I am going to do now. I'm going to fight Will one last time. But we've fought before, and that's all it will be. Maybe he'll whip me again. Maybe I'll whip him. But I'll make you one promise, Sydney, though it is the only one I can make. I won't draw a gun on him."

He wheeled his horse and rode off. She stared after him for an instant, then she gathered up her skirt and started to run.

III

It did not take long for word to spread that Brad was back in Cimarron, and that he had entered Will Kane's home unannounced.

That was just what Brad had counted on.

Brad rode slowly toward the livery at the far end of town. People were pouring out of homes and businesses and walking after him.

When he reached the corral, he swung down and tied his horse with a slip knot. He removed his hat and brushed back his hair with his hand. It was wet with sweat and nerves. He put his hat back on, but tilted it back just far enough to allow him to see clearly—and to give him an air of haughtiness, cockiness. He looked down the long main street toward the bank. Nobody stood in front of it. Nobody seemed to be coming or going.

Inside the blacksmith's shed Brad could hear iron on iron as the smithy worked. He breathed in the pungent but also almost sweet smell of coal burning. Black smoke rose from the forge's chimney.

Brad walked around his horse and pretended to inspect his horse's legs. Walking slowly, running his hands over the animal and down its legs one by one, inspecting each hoof. He had, of course, done this before now. There was nothing wrong with this animal or its shoes. Brad was just trying to make it look like this scene was not being as carefully choreographed as it in fact was.

Down the street he heard Sydney's voice. "Will! Will, Brad's back in town!"

Brad could not hear any more of what they said, but less than a minute later Will Kane came out the front door of the Sheriff's Office, looked down the street, saw Brad, and walked quickly his way.

Brad told me later he had to fight back an impulse to step up and thrust out his hand, or even give him a big bear hug. He liked this man. He had always liked him.

But over Will's shoulder Brad could see the bank, so he set aside those feelings and said what he had to say, something he knew would make Will angry: "That's a nice house you got, Will. I enjoyed my visit with Sydney. Hope I didn't leave any mud in that parlor of yours."

"What do you want, Brad? I take it this isn't a social call?"

"Well, in a manner of speaking, I guess it is. I thought it was about time I came back to Cimarron and gave you a chance to apologize for taking my life from me."

"I should throw you in jail," Will Kane said.

"For what?" Brad said. "I've done nothing wrong in Cimarron except to be your friend on the day you had to prove you were man enough to be sheriff of this dirty little town. I'll admit that was a mistake. A big one. But it's not one I'll make again."

Men were gathering around, eager not to miss a word, or a blow. Brad could not keep his eyes from wandering up the street. He could see a man dismounting a horse near the bank. The man was Hondo.

"Is that why you came back? To even the score?" Will asked.

"No. Like I said. I came back so you could apologize. But if I have to beat one out of you, I guess that would be all right, too."

Sydney was behind Will, and so he added this, to push him over the edge: "I want to show your wife how her pretty boy looks with his hair all mussed up."

Will Kane flushed, but Brad could tell he wasn't completely buying it, either. He looked around at the crowd, and for a second Brad thought he might turn around and look back down the street toward the bank. Hondo was inside, and no horses out front, but Brad was worried. If Will started thinking, he might put two and two together.

Brad couldn't give him time to do the math.

"What's the matter, Will? Has marriage slowed you down? Don't tell me you're getting fat in the belly as well as the head?"

Kane's head spun on a swivel and his hard gaze settled on Brad. "I never backed away from a fight, and you know it."

"You know, Will, I'll grant you that. The Will Kane I used to know never shied away from hard work, or a fight, if it came to that. But that was a long time ago. I'm not sure the man standing in front of me today is that Will Kane. Are you going to hide behind your badge? If I hit a lawman, then you will have reason to throw me in jail." Brad threw up his hands. "I'm carrying no gun. Why don't you take that badge off and fight me man-to-man?"

Even as he said it, Brad knew his words were a lie. This was not man-to-man. It was boy-to-boy. In fact, Brad was betting that Will was not quite man enough to say no to this challenge.

And he knew he had a winning bet when Will's face darkened angrily. He took half a step forward, his fist cocked.

Brad backed away. "Not here, Will."

Brad looked down the street to the bank. A man with a green eye shade and sleeve garters—the banker, a lanky man named Bob Knox—stood in the door. Wheeling around, Brad started down the street toward the corral. Will and the crowd followed.

Brad hung his jacket over his saddle-horn when he reached the corral. He could hear Will arguing with Sydney. But even she knew that Will's mind was made up. This fight would happen.

Turning into Zimmer's feed lot, he put his horse where he

could easily get to it, and faced around to meet Kane. His mouth was dry and his stomach felt empty.

Watch that right, he warned himself. Watch his right and keep moving. Don't let him get set.

A woman Brad remembered as Mrs. Dodd came alongside Sydney and put her hand on Sydney's arm, in part to comfort Sydney, but also in part—it seemed to Brad—to hold her back.

"You just step back," Mrs. Dodd said. "I'll not deny it will be a fight, and I for one have been looking forward to seeing it. From my point of view, it's about time."

"But Will..." Sydney started to protest.

"A fight never hurt a man, Sydney Kane. And it's made more than a few. Buck up, woman."

Mrs. Dodd looked at Brad. "So this is what it comes to." Then, after a beat: "Yes, I guess it does."

Will Kane took off his coat and his guns and hung them on the fence. He turned now and moved toward Brad. But Brad could see in his eyes that his mind was working. He looked around at the crowd. His eyes settled on Bob Knox the banker, who had rushed down the street, leaving his bank unattended, and Brad knew that if he gave Will even a second more he would connect the dots.

So he would not give Will that second. He stepped forward quickly and slapped Will Kane across the mouth.

IV

Hondo dismounted in front of the saloon. He was a big man, but not fat, so when he drew himself up he could be imposing, threatening. But like Brad, who was now playing his own role at the other end of the street, Hondo knew his part, too. It was not the intimidating man he needed to play just now. That would capture and hold the attention of the banker, and perhaps keep him from heading off down the street. No, Hondo needed to play the role of the soft and slouchy man looking for a cool spot out of the sun, always thinking of a way to get out of doing work.

He walked into the bank, brushing by the banker and the cashier standing in the door. They were looking toward the corral, trying to decide whether it was prudent to head down the street and join the crowd, or stay at their posts in the bank. Not a man was in sight this side of the corral, anywhere along the street.

Hondo pulled out a twenty-dollar gold piece. "I'd like some change for this, mister."

Reluctantly, the cashier turned from the door and walked back into the bank. Two riders on dusty horses—Romney and Jeffcoat—drew up before the bank just then and one of them got down. Through the window Hondo saw Romney starting for the door.

The banker turned from the door. "Billy, can you keep an eye on things for a minute? I'm going to check on the commotion down by the livery."

"Sure, boss," the cashier said, with some resignation and disappointment in his voice. "Let me know how it turns out," he said, but the banker was already out the door. Before he can close it, though, Romney steps in, pushes it shut, and locks it from the inside with a twist.

Hondo pulls out a gun and points it at the startled cashier. Soon enough, though, the cashier composes himself.

"Great," the cashier says with resignation. "I miss the fight and get robbed to-boot." He raises his hands. "Nothing here worth dying for, boys. This is payroll money, and the insurance will cover it. Take what you want, but I'm going to need a drink after this. Do you mind leaving me enough for that?"

Romney let out a little snort of a laugh.

Hondo slid through a swinging door, moving behind the teller's wicket. Moving swiftly but carefully, he picked up the neat stacks of banded bills, and he swept the gold into first one sack, then another when the first got too heavy. Hondo could not keep from letting out a low whistle as the sacks filled up and he had to quickly scramble in the cabinets for another pouch. "This is some payday," he said to himself, but loud enough for Romney to hear.

From down the street came the sound of shouts and wild

cheering.

They wasted no motion. No hesitation. As Hondo stripped the counters and safe of the gold, Romney bound and gagged the cashier—not tightly, just enough to keep him quiet and in one place till the fight was over and they came back and discovered him. Then he picked up the sacks and the pilfered pouch—also filled to near bursting—and the two men went out into the street, where Jeffcoat waited, the reins of both their horses in hand.

"Hondo," Romney said, "I'd sure like to see that fight."

"So would I. There's only one thing I'd like to see more. Myself. Alive in Mexico. With my share of this money. So don't think about the fight. Let's ride."

They walked their horses slowly for the first block. If anyone happened to turn their way, they wouldn't see anything out of the ordinary. Just a few strangers who had wandered into town. They turned down the alley they had picked out in advance and began to trot as soon as all three horses were out of sight of the crowd gathered at the corral. At the edge of town, they spurred their horses to a lope.

As they rode south away from the Cimarron River, the ground sloped upward for a mile or more. They kept a good pace till they got to the last spot they could look back and see the town. There was no pursuit.

"I hope he makes it," Romney said. "I surely hope he does."

"He'll make it."

Jeffcoat said nothing at all. He liked the weight of the sack he was carrying, and he was already thinking of Mexico.

Chapter 9

That slap across the mouth had just the effect Brad knew it would. If he had raised his fists, or even sucker-punched him, Will would have taken it as a show of respect. But to be slapped like a girl… Brad knew it would drive Will to fury, and make him instantly forget what might have been worrying him about seeing the banker at the edge of the crowd.

Will's anger caused him to move in swiftly, too swiftly. Brad sidestepped to the right and swung his left arm with his full weight behind it. Will ran directly into it. Blood started spurting from his nose. But for all the spectacle, the blow was not enough to knock him out. Brad was right-handed, and he'd been thrown off enough horses that his left shoulder was all but shot. Will knew that, and he didn't let the blood startle him. He just used the force of Brad's punch to stop his momentum, and returned roundhouse for roundhouse, but Will Kane used his right hand and landed a blow that caused Brad to stumble backwards.

The fight was now well begun, and the crowd bellowed its approval at the opening blows. The two men went into each other slugging. But they were body blows with nothing much on the punches. Little more than wrestling, really. That was fine with Brad, since he knew he had to make the fight last, and it wouldn't have taken too many punches like the ones they started with for this match to be over fast.

As they were groping around, though, Brad's foot rolled and he started to fall. That put just enough space between them for Will to wind up and land a wicked right that caused lights to explode in Brad's brain. Brad went down, but he had just enough sense to roll away from Will. Though it was not a particularly hot day, and they had been fighting for only a couple of minutes, both men were drenched with sweat, and when Brad stopped rolling he was covered in dirt and soot that had landed in the corral from the blacksmith forge, and sand and horse manure and whatever else would stick to him. He got quickly to his feet, but the crowd had stopped cheering and started laughing. Even Will Kane couldn't suppress a smile.

And that infuriated Brad.

It was his turn to move in fast, but even in his fury he did not forget his goal—to keep Will Kane and the crowd on this end of town until his boys were long gone. So Brad did not punch, he landed a shoulder in Will's stomach, and they both hit the ground hard, though Will hit the ground first, and harder, and had the breath knocked out of him.

Brad rolled to the side and slowly got to his feet while Will caught his breath. After that tumble, Will too was covered in a thin crust of blood and sweat and dust and soot. He slowly got to his feet, with a wary eye on Brad.

Will, even in his stunned condition, was surprised. He knew Brad was nothing if not a good finisher. He had seen his former partner fight more than once, and when a man was down, Brad and Will both knew that was the time to finish him off.

What was going on?

There was an angry scrape on Brad's cheekbone, a cut that trickled blood at the corner of his mouth. Will's nose had clotted up, but his face was bloody and his shirt ruined. Both men circled each other, more cautious now. Brad had calmed down, and he had no reason to stretch this fight out any longer. He had done what he had promised his men he would do. It was time to fight to the finish—win or lose.

But Will moved in first, swiftly. He feinted with his left and swung with his right, hoping to catch the point of Brad's chin as he dodged the feint. But Brad was both too quick—and slick with sweat. Will's fist slid off of Brad's face, though the sand and grit scraped the skin off both Brad's face and Will's fist. Still, they fought toe to toe, slugging, smashing, driving. Will landed a left to the side of Brad's face. He bored in, ducking his head, then charging in, but Brad backed up, and none of Will's punches did much damage.

Both men gasped for breath, facing each other. Brad did not mind if the time passed. He would let Will Kane make the next move, which he did. Will moved in and swung a left. But they were both so tired that the fist came in slowly, and Brad didn't dodge it. He grabbed Will's arm by the wrist, pivoted and bent over, and threw Will over his shoulder. Will hit the ground, but he had seen Brad use that move before, and he was ready for it. Will hit the ground in a roll.

On his feet again, Will moved back in, and again the two men pounded each other until they were both streaming with sweat and every man and woman in the crowd was hoarse from shouting. Their arms were so heavy that none of the punches were very hard, but—by the same token—they were both so heavy on their feet that it wouldn't have taken much to knock either man down. So it was no surprise when Will caught Brad with a right with just enough force to knock him off his feet.

Brad hit the ground hard, shaken by the fall. For a second, it looked like Brad might not get up. He took his time rising to his feet. Once upright again, he wiped his face, then wiped his hands on his jeans, and started to walk in again. But Will rushed him and slammed him into the corral fence. This time Brad lost his breath, crumbling to his knees at the base of one of the fence posts.

Will came in to finish him. He wound up his right arm and prepared to land a crushing blow to Brad's face, but in the final instant Brad stood up and brought with him an upper cut that caught Will's chin with Brad's full weight.

Brad's head was buzzing. The roaring of the crowd and the

roaring in his skull seemed one and the same. He got up, and Will charged him. Brad met him with a right to the jaw that smashed Kane full length on the ground.

Will was instantly out, and fell like a sack of flour.

In spite of his exhaustion, panic flooded Brad. Where was his gang? How much time had passed? It certainly felt like enough time. It had felt like a lifetime, in fact. But in such moments, seconds seem like hours. Brad knew this, and while he could take some satisfaction in knowing he had knocked Will out, his own mind was not all that clear itself.

Brad collapsed to his knees. Then he sat down flat in the dirt and sand and soot and manure. The crowd stood silent enough to hear Will Kane groan, and then roll over on his back. Brad and Will looked each other in the eye.

And then Brad wearily put his hand on Will's chest, and he closed his eyes and smiled. Will smiled, too, and slowly lifted himself up to a sitting position, leaning against Brad for balance.

From somewhere in the crowd, someone yelled, "Go fetch these boys some water."

In an instant Sydney was standing over them, her arms akimbo staring down at them both.

"You've had your fight," she said in a tone that could only be described as a scold. "And I'd say it was about even up."

A couple of men stepped up and helped Will to his feet. After a second he steadied himself and reached a hand down to Brad. Brad grabbed it and tried to stand up, but he nearly pulled Will over on top of him. A dozen hands reached in to steady them. Brad and Will stood there, their hands still gripped together tightly.

Brad spoke first. "It was a good fight, Will. Thanks for that, anyway." Then, after a second, "You won't be seeing me anymore. I will leave you and Sydney and Cimarron for good."

Someone grabbed his jacket and hat from the corral fence post and handed it to him. He put his hat on, but not his jacket, and walked over to his horse. He missed the stirrup with his foot the first time, then made it. The crowd parted as he rode slowly through. More than one of the men touched the brim of his hat in a cowboy salute.

Not too fast now, he warned himself.

As he rode past the bank he saw a sign hung on the closed door: "Out to Lunch."

Brad smiled at that touch. He had not told them to put the out-to-lunch sign on the door. But it was a good idea. It would keep everyone out of the bank for maybe as much as a half-hour more. It would hold them all off except the banker himself. He would come back to the bank and let himself in with his own key, though he might stop and talk about the fight for a while.

His head ached and his jaw was stiff. He spat blood into the dust and swore, and even the swearing hurt. Will always could punch. Luckily, Brad's hands were in good shape. They were puffed and swollen but unbroken. Now he worked his fingers to keep the stiffness from them.

The last buildings of the town fell behind, and he lifted the horse to a trot. Horses like to trot. They can cover a lot of ground without getting tired at that gait. But it's tough on the rider, especially a rider that has just had the beating of his life. So Brad nudged the horse to a lope. It's faster, easier on the rider, but not a pace a horse can keep up for long. When he was out of sight of town he ran the horse for half a mile, then slowed to a more moderate pace.

Twice he looked back from high points along the road—the Santa Fe Trail, now the road to Rayado. But he could see no one pursuing, though he knew they would be, so he continued to push his horse. After four miles, which he covered in less than a half-hour, he came to the base of the Tooth of Time, a huge granite monolith that had been a landmark on the old trail. He turned off the main road and headed southwest, following a trail in the wide pasture along the south side of the Tooth.

He continued to push his horse as much as he dared. When he came to Lover's Leap, a large outcropping along the South Urraca Creek, he had gone only ten miles, but he'd gained nearly 2,000 feet in elevation. Just before his trail disappeared into the high country, he paused to look back one last time. He could see for 25 miles off to the east, and what he was looking for was the dust cloud along the base of the Tooth of Time that would tell him that a posse was coming his way.

But he saw none. Surely by now they had figured out the bank had been robbed, but he had the perfect alibi—he was with the sheriff. Some folks, maybe even Will Kane himself, would suspect Brad had led the gang that robbed the Raton Bank. But no one had seen them, and already there was a legend growing that the Raton Bank had been robbed by ghosts.

All of this would have made a fast chase by Will and his posse impossible. Everyone had seen Brad ride out of town alone. Even if they caught him, they would have nothing. No, the best guess for finding the robbers was to head north into the Valle Vidal, where the Raton robbers had fled, or west up Cimarron Canyon, maybe to Blackjack's Hideout or beyond. So Will would have to talk and think and plan before he could head out after Brad. It was one more part of Brad's plan that gave him an advantage, an even greater head start.

As Brad passed Lover's Leap on the old trapper's trail to Taos, he began to pick up the trail of his men. Not that he needed a trail. He knew where he was going, and so did they, and if he didn't catch them before they got to Lookout Meadow, they would wait for him there.

It had gone well, almost too well, yet he felt no elation. He had gotten back at the town that had thrown him under the wagon, so to speak, but he took no pleasure in it. The whole escapade left a bitter taste in his mouth. Yes, he had gotten away, and he was anxious to see what sort of a haul they had made. There would be some thrill in that, assuming the number was big enough.

But he was now on the run, and this would be a long, hard run to Mexico. Four hundred miles through rough country, avoiding towns and nearly killing their horses along the way, certainly having to abandon them at least once to spend some of their booty on fresh mounts.

An altogether distasteful business.

Yes, he was still free, and in a couple of hours he would know if he was rich, but what sort of freedom is it when every sheriff in the country is hunting for you?

The trail grew steep as he climbed higher into the Sangre de Cristo Mountains. He came to a high pass, Fowler Pass, Brad had heard it called: over 9,000 feet. It was now late afternoon, and Brad was sure they were on his trail by now. Even if they had sent parties west and north, Brad knew Will Kane would not rest if there were any doubt that he had been involved in the bank hold-up.

But Brad also knew that even if they were in pursuit, it would be nearly dark when they got to Fowler Pass. And that last climb would take the starch out of more than a few of them. And there was no water up this high. Fowler Pass would be the end of the trail for many in the posse.

He led his horse down into the high mountain valley beyond Fowler Pass. This was Bonito Canyon, and a creek ran down the lowest part. He dismounted, stripped off his shirt, and quickly and imperfectly washed off some of the grime of the fight and the ride. He rode down the canyon for a mile before taking another steep uphill trail to Lookout Meadow, where Rye Burns had four fresh horses waiting for them.

He saw Hondo as soon as he came into the edge of the meadow. His horse was spent, but it perked up at the smell of the other horses and Brad trotted him the last few hundred yards to where the others waited on the high side of the meadow.

Brad swung to the ground, and Romney moved in quickly and switched his saddle to his own horse for him.

Hondo stared at Brad's face, not able to hide his shock, but all he could say was, "How'd it go?"

Brad's face was puffed and he now had two blackened eyes. His nose and lips had not completely stopped bleeding. He had stopped even bothering to wipe the blood away, licking it away instead, which made his lips and tongue red. He just stared at Hondo for a few seconds, then said, "I told you he could punch."

Hondo looked away and Brad's eyes searched for the bags with the money from the bank. "Just tell me it was worth the trouble."

"Oh, you're damned right it was," Romney blurted out. "We filled the two bags we brought and one more we grabbed at the bank. How much do you think that is? Did we get the whole sixty-thousand?"

Hondo had a look of mild disgust on his face. "Don't jinx us," he said. "Let's ride. We can do the counting later."

They stepped into their saddles and started out. Brad knew this country. They knew what they had to do. They turned loose the horses they had ridden this far. They were all four spent, and all they did was put their heads down to start munching on the spotty grass clumps in the meadow, but eventually they would drift back to Rayado, where Rye had gotten them, or get roped somewhere along the way.

Brad was bone tired, and his weariness was as much mental as physical. They had just pulled off the biggest score of their lives. One of the biggest scores any of them had ever heard of. And no one even knew their names. If they could get away, it would be one for the history books. Brad knew that. They all did.

But getting away, that was a big "if."

They were well into the mountains now, and the views behind them were few, but every time they came to a rise they looked back. So far, nothing in sight. After yesterday's rain, though, there wouldn't be a lot of dust. Still, a posse wouldn't be that hard to see, even from a distance, and even though they could see nothing, and even though no one had seen them rob the bank, they had the bags of money. If they got caught with it, they were dead men. They had even talked about ditching the money somewhere along the way and coming back for it later, but decided against that. They were now on fresh, fast horses. There was nothing to do now but to ride as hard and as far as these horses would carry them, and either buy or steal four more.

Still, Brad worried about Will. The fight was Brad's alibi. It was proof positive he didn't rob the bank, but Will would have no doubt that he had been played, and he would be mad. And he wouldn't be the only one in Cimarron who would be mad. Some might think that Brad had finally gotten even, and might even admire Brad for pulling off such an elegant stunt. Some might even think it was a good joke. But it would stop being funny when they realized how much money was gone. And joke or no joke, they would all join in, and any one of them would run him down and shoot him like a rabid dog if they ever caught him.

His face throbbed with every step of his horse. It was puffed and bruised and cut. Sweat trickled into the cuts, and the salt stung and burned. But the pain was manageable, and they were on fresh horses. So, at least for a few minutes, he let his mind think through what they had just pulled off. He had finally made his grubstake. He could stop outlawing forever. He had gotten back at the people who had wronged him. He had taken back wages and then some. More than that, he had humiliated them.

But none of it brought him any joy whatsoever.

"Oh, dear God," Brad thought. "What have I done?"

Chapter 10

Hondo saw the smoke first, as soon as they rode out of the trees and into the vast high meadow of Wildhorse Park. "Now what in the…?" His voice trailed off as they all saw the billowing cloud rising ahead of them.

"I hope that ain't what it looks like," Romney said. "I left my girl's picture in that store. I'd hate to see it get burned up."

They slowed their pace to a near stop. One by one, but in quick succession, the men yanked their rifles from their scabbards. Brad swung wide on the flank and a little in advance. Jeffcoat wheeled to the right, the uphill side, and climbed above the compound of buildings to see if he could look down into the plaza. They came up to the buildings in a slow walk, warily.

The store was gone. Only the adobe walls of one building remained, probably the way Rye Burns had found it, long ago.

"Tracks," Romney said, indicating them. "Fire still burning. They can't be gone very long."

"He got one," Jeffcoat said, pointed to a large patch of blood.

Brad rode around quickly to see. But there was no body.

"Didn't kill him," Brad said. "At least not yet. But I'm guessing he won't get far after losing that much blood."

"Not just one," Romney said. "Burns must have made a real fight of it," Romney said. "I'd never have believed he had it in him. He must have killed three, by the look of things. The one they carried off, and here's two more here."

They all gathered around, but none of them dismounted. One body, an Anglo, had fallen face down right at Burns' feet. His jacket had a hole in the back where the bullet had exited.

"Shot through the heart," Hondo said.

Another was just a few feet away, the right side of his face blown nearly off by what was likely a shotgun blast at close range.

They had been coming for Burns, and it looked like they killed him just as Burns got off the shots that killed them. Brad's gang could not take time to bury him, and Burns would have been the first to understand that. Let the posse do it.

Romney jumped down off his horse and ran into the ruins of the bar. Seconds later he came out.

"Whoever it was took all the liquor, but here's a couple of bags of coffee." He tossed them up to Hondo, who tied them together with a short piece of string and slung them over his saddlebags, which were already bulging.

Romney mounted and they rode out swiftly to the south, following the trail of whoever had done this—not by design, but because they were headed the same way.

They went down the trail at a walk, all of them seeing the tracks of the marauders who killed Rye Burns. There were enough of them that the tracks just blended together. Eight? Ten? More?

But occasionally they could see the tracks Papa and I had left. The marauders would surely have seen our tracks, too, and they would know one of the riders was a woman. A good tracker would know which horse I rode.

None of this was lost on Brad and his men. They knew what was ahead of him: Papa and me, followed by maybe as many as a dozen renegades.

But at that time we did not know what was behind us. Yes, Papa was no tenderfoot. He had been "up the crick and over the pass," as the boys along the Front Range were fond of saying. And for that matter, so had I. My year living with Papa had not been in vain. I knew enough to pay attention to Papa and the things he paid attention to, and I could handle a rifle better than most of the men we were likely to encounter along the trail.

Still, Brad could see that he was about to come face to face with a dilemma. Should he stick to his plan and head to Mexico in the fastest way possible, or should he follow us?

It was very hot. The air was still. Brad and his boys rode at a good pace, conserving the strength of their horses, yet keeping up a steady, distance-eating gait.

The original plan was still good, and they were still following it. They would head south through the Pecos Mountains, which is what they called the southernmost reaches of the Sangre de Cristos. When they came alongside Santa Fe, they would head east out of the mountains, then due south as fast as they could go through the very heart of the deserts of southern New Mexico until they reached Mexico. It would be three hundred grueling miles, and they would have to avoid towns. They had been careful to cut the telegraph wires to the south as they rode into town, but it wouldn't take more than half a day for that to get fixed. This robbery would be on the front page of the *Albuquerque Daily Journal*, almost for sure, and within a day or two, at most.

Water was not a problem now. The rain of the night before had re-charged many of the kettle ponds and creeks running through the bottoms of the canyons. But the farther south they went past Santa Fe, the harder it would be to find good water. That could be their death, but also their salvation. If water was hard for them to find, it would be just as hard for their pursuers, and more discouraging, since whoever was chasing them—if they were even still chasing them by then—would have to turn around and return home through that same inhospitable country. Brad was counting on finding *tinajas*—depressions in the rock that would fill with water during rains. *Tinajas* could keep a few men alive in desert country—but likely not a posse.

II

Brad told me later he gave no thought to the money in the sacks they carried. He told me he was thinking only of me, and Papa, and the renegades and outlaws on the trail between us.

But Papa and I did not know yet that we were about to be in a fight for our lives. Sure, there had been a few surprises, Brad Bradshaw not least among them, but he had been no threat to us. As far as I knew then, this was still just a scenic ride through the high country, the mountain route to Santa Fe.

I could tell, though, that Papa was increasingly on edge. At the time, I thought it was because he had caught Brad and me together and he didn't know what to say—or do—about it.

Now that I am an old woman I know what was in his mind, and it was a hard question: Could I be trusted? It is a question you don't want to ask of your own daughter, and maybe few fathers will admit to asking it, but Papa had been asking that very question, and he had come to the only answer he could allow himself, the only answer that love would allow. He would trust me. After all, when a girl got to be the age I was then, and especially—Papa admitted this to himself with some bitterness—especially when he had been around so little.... He had no choice but to trust me.

But could he trust Brad? Every bit of trail-side rumor he had heard said that Brad Bradshaw was a gentleman. That is, if you don't count the fact that he was an outlaw.

"I am not much of a father," Papa said suddenly. "I never understood women or pretended to. Your Ma was different. She knew how to handle me, but I just do the wrong things, Ali. You've got to make allowances."

This was Papa's way of apologizing to me for the previous evening. A part of me wanted to put him out of his misery, to be more mature than I was, and say, "That's alright, Papa. Don't you worry about anything you said or did. I know you love me and I love you, too."

But we did not talk to each other that way, at least not back then. So I said nothing, and Papa searched for words as we rode through the hot, still afternoon.

"Had your Ma lived, she would have wanted you to marry a good man and have a home, and that's what I want for you."

We rode on. It was only a few hours ago that the rain had

ceased, but there was little indication of it except for some cracked mud in the bottom of a hollow here and there. Still, Papa's alertness told me he wasn't worried about water. He wiped his rifle free of dust, then bit off a chew of tobacco. Whatever Papa was thinking, all he said was, "Next shade, we'll pull up a bit."

Papa didn't have to say so, but I knew. We needed to keep our horses fresh. There was no telling when we might have to run for it.

Suddenly, in front of us, we saw tracks that came up from the plains to the east. The tracks cut across our trail. Six horses, and the tracks were not an hour old.

Papa studied their trail, looked off in the direction they were riding, but saw nothing.

"No telling who they are," he said. "They might just be a bunch of cowboys headed for Taos. But we'd better take care."

We were vulnerable, of course, the two of us riding alone. But we were also not much of a threat to anyone. Aside from our horses and rifles, we didn't have much to steal. I would not let myself entertain the notion that a bunch of marauding men who had not seen a woman in a while might consider me prize enough. If Papa had that thought he did not say anything, though I'm sure if he did have that thought his conclusion would have been the same as mine. They would have to kill me first.

It would not take long for anyone we encountered to come to that conclusion as well. So as long as we stayed out of everyone's way, it seemed likely we could pass through safely.

We rode on through this spectacular country. It was not a pure wilderness. There were trails and occasionally even a rough wagon road. We would follow it if it went our way, but it would inevitably turn east toward the plains or west toward the Rio Grande Valley, and we would leave it to stay in the high country. We were well south of Taos now, and we would occasionally break out of the forest into a high mountain meadow, sometimes surrounded by rimrock, or we would scramble up a rockfall onto a high mountain cirque or up a canyon wall where we could ride for a few miles with unobstructed views of mountains still covered in snow. From time to time we could make out the gash in the land off to the west, that gash marking the Rio Grande, which cut a path parallel to our route at least for now—due south—then east for hundreds of miles, eventually emptying into the Gulf of Mexico.

"This is what I wanted you to see, Ali," Papa said. "I know there are beautiful mountains in California, and the ocean, but...." His voice trailed off.

We rode on in silence, taking in nothing but the mountains and the plains and the sky until the trail turned upward and into the trees again.

"Papa?"

"Huh?"

"Bradshaw and the others. Do you think they made it?"

"No tellin'."

"Will they come this way?"

"Maybe." Then, after a beat or two, "I expect they will. They headed up into the mountains to throw off the posse chasing them from Cimarron, but it won't take long for the word to get out to Taos and Santa Fe and even Albuquerque and points south. They'll have to take to the desert and ride hard and fast. There's nothing like a desert to take the starch out of a posse. So, yeah, they might come this way, but they'll head out of the mountains either east or west and then make as straight a line as they can for Mexico."

The question caused Papa to turn in his saddle and look behind him. But the trail behind us was empty, and we saw no dust beyond. The idea that Brad might be coming this way excited my mind. Should we stop and wait for them? No, that was a foolish idea. Even if they did come this way, they would not want us riding with them, and we were headed toward town, which is precisely where they did not want to be.

So we kept riding, though Papa could not ride easy. He kept twisting and turning. He could not shake the feeling we were being watched, but we could see nothing. The smoke signal we had seen earlier was just so unusual in this part of the country. It was mostly a lost skill, and a Plains Indian skill at that. But there it was. No mistaking it.

Papa came from a time and place where you didn't trust Indians. He did not like the idea that they might be able to see him and he couldn't see them. His attitude was, once you had Apaches on your trail, you were in trouble until you got to safety or they decided you weren't worth their trouble. And it didn't matter much to him that the people out there watching us—if they were watching us—were probably not even Indians, or at least mostly Indians. The Jicarilla Apache had been moved to a reservation down in the southern part of the state.

Indian or not, Papa was right to be on the lookout for bad guys—whoever they were. It seemed unlikely they would attack. What made us vulnerable in some ways kept us safe. Sure, I was a young girl and Papa was an old man, but even a roving band of outlaws, opportunists, would know that killing us would bring every gun in New Mexico down on them.

Besides, this was not country easy to hide in. When we dropped low into the canyons, the trees opened up into meadows or semi-arid brush country and we could see from canyon wall to canyon wall. Up high the trees were thin. Someone would have to pick his spot carefully for us not to know he was there, and if a group tried to rush us, they must know we would be armed, too. We could dismount and take steady shots from the ground. If enough of them came at us at once, we would not survive, but we could take more than a few of them with us.

It was a gruesome calculation, but it did work in our favor, even if it took some of the joy out of this last ride down the spine of New Mexico.

It didn't take all the joy, though. As tense as we were, the beauty of the place pressed in on us. I did not hate Texas, and I would grow to love California, especially the ocean. But the Sangre de Cristo Mountains of New Mexico are like no other place on earth. In later years we would come back to New Mexico and hear some of the younger folk call it a heaven on earth. I could not quite go that far. For one thing, I hoped for more out of heaven and—for another—the place held too many memories of death.

But even that possibility of death was part of the place's terrible beauty. It was a real place. Hard and awesome. If you tested yourself against this place, and passed the test, you were…well, you had accomplished something significant.

But, again, I get ahead of myself. In that moment, on that hot day in July of 1881, mostly what I thought about was to keep going. If someone was following us, as Papa clearly thought, we would likely be safe till dark, and when we did finally stop, we could choose our spot, a spot to take a stand if taking a stand became necessary.

And whatever dangers were out there, over the past year I had come to feel safe with Papa, safe enough to ask him a question that had been pent up in me for months. "Papa. How did you meet my mother?"

Preoccupied as he was with staying alert, the question startled him, and I could see that it even annoyed him a bit. But the question, coming as it did so out-of-the-blue, and at such a time… Papa could see that it was a question I had wanted to ask for a while, and one that he must have known deserved an answer.

But he did not answer right away. I could almost see the gears in his head spinning as he tried to figure out what I was really asking. Did I really want to know how they met? No, that's not why anyone asks such questions. I didn't want to know who she was so much as I needed to know who I was, and my question was a way to that answer.

"Oh," Papa began tentatively. "Before the war broke out, your mother married a Union man in Tennessee. Being a Union man from a secesh state was no easy row to hoe. But he was a preacher, of sorts. No, not a preacher like the kind who led a church. But he would go around the countryside preaching.

"He was a gunsmith by trade and I guess he could have made a fortune selling and repairing guns, but he was an abolitionist, and a peaceful man. Not one to push his views on others, but not one to be pushed around, either. He couldn't fight for Tennessee, and he wouldn't fight against his neighbors. So they came west to Texas, hoping to outrun the war, I guess....

"I knew him a bit. He was a good man. The kind of man your mother deserved."

Papa fell silent for a long minute, but after a bit he continued.

"He took to preaching again around Tyler. Gunsmithin' during the week, and he would ride a circuit around the low country there preaching on Saturday night in one town, then Sunday morning in another, and Sunday night in a third and ride hard to get back home by midnight. He drove himself hard, too hard. He took a fever and died."

Papa paused for a long minute. I began to think that this was all he was going to tell me for now, but he continued. "Like I said, I knew him some. I had fought in the war and then drifted down into Texas. And it was during that time that I was not doing too well. The war, I guess. And I had started drinking by then. But I would talk with him, and it helped.... The war had killed something in me, I guess you could say, and talking with him helped it come back to life. But then he died, too."

Another long minute passed in silence. "But after he died, and since I was around, I sort of stopped by, time to time, to see how your mother—she wasn't your mother then, of course—was making out. And we would talk about her husband. We both loved him, I guess, and that's what brought us together.

"Your Ma was a real lady. Educated. She made me promise to see that you got some schooling.

"I never quite figured out what she saw in me. I was younger then, a'course, and maybe handsome. I don't know. I was certainly fit, and I could work a long day. Maybe not so crotchety as I've become. Anyway, I grew to love your mother, and over time she grew to love me, and it was then, I guess, that I learned what a difference love could make.

"We had a good life. Especially after you came along and for a few years after that."

"I don't really remember."

"Really? None of it?"

"Just a few odd things. I remember her holding me and reading to me by the fire at night. But I don't remember her being sick."

Papa's eyes had not stopped moving as he talked, but both of us were fixed on the horizon, and we missed what was right alongside of us: a rattler coiled up on a rock ledge on the uphill side of the trail. I had been riding in front, so by the time it rattled I was alongside it and more or less at eye level.

Now, most horses are not that afraid of rattlesnakes. Not as afraid as they should be, if you ask me. Too often they are more curious than afraid and go snooping around. The few horses I ever heard of getting bit by rattlesnakes got bit on the nose.

And I'm not much afraid of rattlers either, having seen plenty of them. But the sound of this one so close to my head gave me a start and I instinctively ducked away, jerking the reins as I went.

On the narrow mountain trail, my sudden jerk was all it took for my little mustang to push his front left foot out to keep its balance. The only problem was, there was no trail there to come down on. We started leaning far out over the steep talus slope that fell to our left. I reached for the saddle horn but my hand landed on the stock of my Winchester rifle. I held on as we went off the edge, headlong down a long rock slide.

I came off the mustang and let go of the reins, though my hand kept a death grip on the rifle, and it slid out of its scabbard as I came off the horse. Later, Papa told me I screamed, but I don't remember that. All I remember was trying to keep the horse from rolling over me as we slid down the steep rock slope.

And I did. I used my free hand to grab a scrub oak that had managed to find a home amid the gravely rockslide. My momentum ripped the tree out of my hand, but it slowed me enough and got my head above my feet. I dug the heels of my boots into the gravel, and after another fifteen or twenty feet, I grabbed another tree and came to a stop.

Papa was off his horse and down the rockslide just seconds behind me. I was already getting up, and though I was covered in dust and scraped up a bit, nothing seemed broken. Still, Papa threw his arms around me and said, "Oh, Ali. Are you okay?"

"I think so, Papa."

Papa continued down the slope to my horse. Even before he reached it he could see that its leg was broken. There was no hope for it. The leg was badly shattered, and for all we knew it had a snake bite too. He stripped off the pack behind the cantle of the saddle, then, not wishing to risk a shot, he stooped quickly and with his Bowie knife cut the horse's throat.

I started toward him, but he raised his hand with the bloody knife in it.

"I'm sorry, but he's gone. His leg's completely shattered. There's nothing else to do."

"Oh, Papa."

For the first time, tears started to fill my eyes. I don't know if the tears were from relief that I had just barely escaped getting killed, or if they were for the horse. But I did say: "He was such a fine horse."

Papa, though, didn't think so. He relieved his anxiety a bit by letting roll a stream of invective against the animal.

"That was a rattle-brained, hammer-headed broom-tail, and never an ounce of good to anybody." He paused. "Nevertheless, we're going to miss him, and that's a fact."

One horse between us now, and likely seventy-five miles of hard country to go before we got to Lamy, the train station just south of Santa Fe.

"We'll make out with one horse," he said when we got back up to the top of the slide.

"We'll have to."

Chapter 11

Things had taken a turn for the worse. We knew that.

For one thing, we had planned to sell these horses when we got to Santa Fe to help pay for the train ticket west. We had other money, and of course we were both willing to work, so losing the horse would not keep us from getting to California. Still, a good horse was worth real money, and watching the blood flow out of that poor dying horse was like watching money flow down the drain.

The real problem, though, was the fact that we would have to get by on just one horse for the next seventy-five or so miles, and those miles through some of the most rugged country in the West.

Papa seemed almost proud of me when he saw I had pulled my rifle out and was hugging it to me when he scrambled down to me. As I said, though, it was not planning or forethought. I was just grabbing whatever I could grab, and the rifle slid out when I came out of the saddle. Still, it was a bit of good luck—if luck is the right word for it. If the horse had rolled over it, it likely would have broken the stock or maybe even bent the barrel and made the gun unusable. More than that, Papa had an unshakable belief in his guns. A man with a gun could protect himself, could feed himself. He could make a way in the world. Such a person was not without hope.

So we were not without hope, or a way forward. But it would be a harder way.

And, of course, what we didn't know then was just how big a mess we were in. We were being chased, or at least followed. Papa had an inkling, of course. And now that we were in our—how shall I call it—reduced circumstances, Papa knew he would need me to be fully alert.

"I've been spotting men on the ridgetops," he said. "And smoke."

"Smoke signals?" I said, with a bit of wonder, actually. Smoke signals seemed quaint in the era of the telegraph. It was something I would not even have known to be on the lookout for. "Are they Indians?"

"Some of them may be," he said. "But renegades and outlaws mostly. White, Indian, Mexican, whatever. Good men come in all colors, and bad ones do, too." I had heard Papa say that many times. He told me it was something Father Dyer used to say.

We did not know then, of course, of the murder of Rye Burns, but Papa said he had been expecting trouble if Brad and his gang had been successful.

"It's easier to ambush and rob a few men up in the mountains than it is to sneak into town and rob a bank. Bradshaw's boys did all the hard work. These renegades'll kill them and take the money."

He let that sink in. Papa must have known that the news disturbed me, so he added, "Well, look at it this way. The fact that they're roaming round for Bradshaw means he must have gotten clean away…and…he got out with a big haul."

I did not find the news comforting, though I did find it fascinating, and was tempted to get lost in those thoughts, though I knew I needed to be on the alert. This Pecos country was wild land, and a million acres of it. More, even. But it was surrounded by country that had become less wild. Santa Fe to the south of us. Taos to the west. Las Vegas to the east, on the edge of the plains. These were real towns with churches and families and—except maybe on Saturday night in the rougher areas—law and order.

So there were faint roads and trails. The one we were following, of course, but also others. We took one of them, a faint trail that led us up a canyon till the canyon closed in around us—sheer walls on our left and right that we could almost reach out and touch at the same time, rising thirty feet on our left, but only head-high or a little more on our right. It was a massive boulder that centuries before had fallen off the side of the canyon wall. We rode around it, and behind it there was a gap in the wall, eroded over the years that allowed us to scramble out of the canyon and into a high mountain meadow not unlike the park in the Valle Vidal where I had first met Brad just a few days before.

"Bear Caves," Papa said. "There are no caves here, but..." and he pointed up, to the rimrock of a mesa a hundred feet overhead. "There are little caves up there, made when these rocks fell."

Boulders formed a jumbled maze along the edge of the meadow nearest the steep side of the mesa.

Night was still a few hours away. Under normal conditions, we would have kept going until nightfall and then found a spot on the side of the trail to camp. But this meadow, tucked against a nearly sheer rock face, was perfect. We found a spot against the mesa that was a bit higher than the meadow and gave us a view of anything that moved out in front of us. To our backs was the mesa wall. No one would sneak up from behind. It was a place the two of us could defend against ten attackers, if we had to. For a while anyway.

We huddled behind a massive boulder that gave us a measure of protection while still allowing us to fully protect our front. We would not build a fire. The plan was to rest here, perhaps even sleep a bit, until it was fully dark, and then quietly continue south. By the time the sun came up, we might even be close enough to Santa Fe to see people again, and relative safety.

But I was too scared, or excited—or both—to sleep. So we sat with our backs to the mesa, sheltered in our little rock fortress, Papa with his eyes on one approach, and me with my eyes on the other. A half hour went by in silence before I said: "Papa?"

"Huh?"

"That Bradshaw…Is he a bad man?"

Now, of course, I know what a loaded question that was. I may have known even then. And even if I did know it was loaded, I still meant it sincerely, honestly, even innocently. What did Papa, a good judge of men, think of this man?

Looking back, I can still see Papa's face as I asked it. I think he knew that the next words out of his mouth might set the course of the rest of my life—provided, of course, that any of us made it out alive, which just three days ago I would not have guessed would be a concern, though it had certainly become one.

He studied the question with care. He told me later that his first impulse was to take the coward's way out—to say that he had plenty to think about with the men who aimed to kill us, or rob us, and that he would think about Brad later.

But there was nothing of the coward left in Papa. At least that's what I thought. Papa, for his part, would say in later years that he was nothing but a coward in those early days when he was outlawing and drinking. It was not bravery or skill, but fear, that turned him into an outlaw.

"Perfect love," he would say, quoting the Bible, "don't cast out hate. It casts out fear." He would say it was Mama's love that helped him get over his fear, though when she died it came back, and it was then that he did most of his outlawing. It was Father Dyer, up in Colorado City, in the year before he called for me, that showed him the way back for good.

But Papa said all this—as I said—in his later years, after he'd read a few books and life had given him time to think on things a bit.

For now, to his credit, he did not run from the question. He answered: "No, Ali. No, he's not. He's an outlaw. I've heard the stories, and I am not saying he don't have his reasons. But the choices were his, and so far he's made some bad ones.

"I will say this, though. He may be a bad man, but he's got the makings of a good man."

I reached over and laid my hand on Papa's arm. And he laid his wrinkled, rough hand on mine. And we sat that way for a long time, and I drifted off to sleep in the afternoon sun.

II

I woke with a start when Papa pulled away from me and brought his Winchester up to shooting position.

"Grab your rifle," Papa hissed in a loud whisper. "And draw your pistol out and lay it down next to you in case you need it quick."

The gray horse—the one we had left—had been exhausted after hauling both of us to this high meadow. Still, we had hobbled him, even though there was little danger he would run off. Now, though, he seemed excited. His head was up, and his ears were alert, moving back and forth to pick up any sound he could.

Suddenly a rabbit bolted out of the woods. It either saw or smelled us, and then veered off sharply away from us, into the rocks.

Papa was listening intently into the stillness, and so was I, but it gave back no sound.

"Something's out there," he said. "A rabbit don't jump like that in this heat unless he's scared."

He squatted on his heels, his Winchester ready. He pulled back on the hammer, to half-cock. Then, grinding his heel into the sand to stifle the sound, to full cock.

He started to turn his head when he heard the scrape of a boot on rock. He turned swiftly on the ball of his right foot, slamming his back against the rocks just as a man dressed in one part buckskin and one part old U.S. Army uniform sprang forward.

The Winchester leaped in Papa's hand, and the man's throat vanished in a red smear as the bullet tore through, ripping the neck wide open.

The sound of the shot slapped against the rock walls, then echoed away and lost itself in the distance.

The body fell within reach of me, and I recoiled at the mess of blood and sinew and bone that had been his face and head.

He was young, and it was hard for me to tell if he was Anglo or Mexican or Apache. Probably an Indian who thought he knew something about stealth and wanted to impress whoever was with him, waiting in the trees at the edge of the meadow.

But we heard nothing.

The dead man carried a Winchester and had a Mexican bandolier filled with cartridges. Papa shucked these from their loops one by one and filled his pockets. The Winchester was old, and this man-child had shown the same irresponsibility in caring for it as he had just now demonstrated, costing him his life.

Still, it looked like it would fire, so Papa levered a shell into the firing chamber and laid it down beside him. It might come in handy.

I pushed the dead man away with my feet, rolling him over so I could not see his face and head.

"He's so young," I whispered, stating the obvious but trying—I guess—to process what I had just seen.

"Old as he will ever be," Papa said dryly.

The matter-of-factness in Papa's voice caught me up short, and it suddenly occurred to me that this was not the first man he had ever killed. Years later he would tell me that he took no pleasure in killing even the worst of men. But he did, he said, take pleasure in staying alive, and one of the skills he had to master to stay alive—at least in those early days—was to learn how to kill.

III

Right about then, a few miles to the north on the trail we had just come, Brad and his men came to the place the rattlesnake had startled me. Brad's gang, all experienced trailmen, had no trouble seeing something had happened there. They looked down to the left of the trail and saw the dead horse we had left behind, with its broken leg and cut throat. They all drew rein and looked down on the dead animal.

The story the scene told was easy enough to figure out. The story it didn't tell, but which Brad and the rest of his men could piece together also easily enough, was that we were now on one horse in wild country, with outlaws close on our trail.

The question now became, what would they—Brad and his men—do about it?

Brad had taken this route through the mountains to take the starch out of the posse that would be following, and to keep them guessing about where they were heading. What he had planned on doing from here was to turn east, onto the plains, and head south through the desert of eastern New Mexico south all the way to Mexico. The way was so scarcely populated, and the rangeland so open, that they could do 100 miles day—if they could get fresh horses once or twice along the way, and with the money they had, getting fresh horses would not be a problem. They would be to Mexico while lawmen and bounty hunters were still looking for them in the mountains around Cimarron.

But what about this? Could Brad just leave Papa and me to the hands of whatever outlaws were chasing us now, especially after seeing what they had done to Rye Burns?

Brad would say later, years later, when he had made his mark in so many different ways, that being able to see what others could not see, or could not see yet, was both a blessing and a curse.

"The curse," he would say, "is that seeing things before others do causes you to act in ways that others don't understand."

But it did not take a prophet to read these signs—just someone with a bit of trail savvy, and Brad and his men had plenty of that. On this day, all Brad said was, "That's Ali's horse."

The four men, loaded with the loot of their robbery, looked at our dead horse and upon those tracks, and all of them read the same story. For each of them, what they saw represented a hard choice, though the choice was different for Brad than for the men in his gang. For Brad, he had to decide whether to abandon his carefully laid plan to save an old man who he wasn't sure was his enemy or not, and a young girl he wasn't sure—then, anyway—was worth the risk.

But from the moment he rode into Cimarron and saw what Will Kane had built with his pretty wife, and had seen what the town had become—no longer an outlaw town, but a town of families and churches and schools.... From that moment till this one, he had vowed to leave the outlaw trail.

But now, here he was, standing over this dead horse, already beginning to bloat up in the heat, with flies buzzing around the sticky blood that had poured out of its neck where Papa had carved a clean slit. This putrid sight was the way of all flesh. It would one day be his fate, too. Could it really be this easy, this clear, this unambiguous. You come to that place where you make an honorable decision or you don't, and everything from then on hangs on that choice?

Brad looked into the eyes of the men riding with him and he could tell they were worried.

"This is one helluva deal," Hondo said.

"It is," Romney agreed. "But it don't concern us. Stanton is one tough pilgrim. Two on one horse ain't my preferred mode of travel, but it's do-able. And we ain't all that far from Santa Fe, if they headed down toward the Rio Grande, out of the mountains."

That was true enough. A day, maybe a little more.

Hondo cleared his throat uneasily. "No time to waste. We'd better push on."

And they did. For a few miles, anyway, they were going the same way we were, so each man thought about the decision he had coming. The sun had gone down, but there was light enough to see—for a while anyway.

"It isn't far to the trail down to Wagon Mound," Brad said. "Let's get along. I don't want to miss that cut-off."

This is where they would abandon the mountains, head east toward the high plains, and then south in a straight line for Mexico.

I don't know what was going on in their minds when Brad said that. Was it relief that they were not abandoning their plan on some quixotic quest to rescue an old man and his daughter? Or were they feeling the same things that were tugging at Brad?

Before long they came on the road to Wagon Mound. It was

hard to see in the dark, but they saw it and without hesitation Brad led the men down the new path to the east. If Hondo, Romney, and Jeffcoat were relieved, they did not say so, they just quietly followed.

But before they got even a quarter-mile toward Wagon Mound, barely out of sight of the southbound trail they had been on, Brad stopped up short.

"I gotta go after them, boys," he said. "They're sitting ducks and don't know it."

"Old Dave Stanton probably knows something," Hondo said. "He's a sharp old man."

Brad considered that. "Yeah, maybe, but even if he knows he's being followed, there's not a lot he can do about it. You saw what they did to Rye Burns. Even if they hole up somewhere, they won't be able to hold them off forever."

No one spoke. They all knew Brad was right. They also knew that if Brad went alone he would likely die with us. Brad knew it, too.

"This is the way it's going to be. I'm going after them. Y'all keep the money. If I get myself killed, I won't be needing it, and if I survive, I'll come find you. You can be damn sure of that. So save me my share."

Hondo let out a suppressed laugh. "We couldn't spend it if we wanted to."

Romney could contain himself no longer. "It must be sixty thousand. Sixty thousand in gold."

The four horsemen grew quiet as that number sank in. For a few seconds they just faced each other in silence, their mounts nose to nose. They were four outlaws riding for the border, four men who had chosen to live by the gun, and someday likely to die by it. Romney wanted a woman in Mexico, and—eventually—a family. Hondo wanted a long, quiet drunk. Jeffcoat wanted nothing at all except to ride with these men, men who had accepted him and given him a reason to live—however flawed or broken that reason might be. For Jeffcoat, it was reason enough.

And what was Brad thinking? He had taken more money

from the Cimarron bank than he thought existed in the whole world—certainly more than enough to settle whatever grievance he thought he had with the town. But it brought him no satisfaction. The gold was a burden to him now, a reminder of a life he now more than anything wanted to leave behind.

But in those few seconds of silence, they all made the same decision. They had ridden with Brad this far. They would go the rest of the way.

Who can say for sure why? They were all well aware that this was the biggest job any of them had ever pulled. Bigger than any job any of them had ever even heard about. And they all three knew that it was Brad who made it happen, made it happen without a shot being fired. Call it loyalty. Call it an unwillingness to give up on the man who had brought them the first bit of good luck any of them had had in a very long time. Call it what you will. But it was settled. Without a word it was settled. They would follow Brad, no matter what.

Jeffcoat suddenly cocked his head. "Horses pass," he hissed in a loud whisper.

"Now how do you know that?" Romney demanded.

"I can taste the dust," Jeffcoat said softly. "And smell the paint. The medicine smell."

"There ain't no fighting Indians in New Mexico anymore," Romney said.

"They're probably just outlaws, but they paint up anyway."

So it was not Will Kane and the posse from Cimarron, just a band of outlaws sensing some easy targets—whether the bank robbers or Papa and me, it was likely all the same to them.

They waited, listening. One of their horses stamped impatiently. But whoever had passed kept riding without noticing in the deepening dark that Brad and his men had turned off the trail. Now, in a stroke of blind luck that no planning could have accounted for, Brad and his men were suddenly the hunters, not the hunted.

They backtracked up the ridge, came back to the trail Papa and I were on, and turned left, south. They did not move quickly, as they did not know if the outlaws ahead of them would keep riding or bed down for the night. And the posse behind them—if it still was behind them—would likely not risk following at night for fear of losing the trail.

Overhead the stars were a gaudy spectacle. It's hard to describe the New Mexico sky. The air is cool and thin at this elevation, and the Milky Way is a white path across a sky so bright—even without a moon—that you can see by it.

The four rode on in silence until Jeffcoat spoke in a forced whisper: "Woodsmoke. They are very near."

No one else said a word. The smoke might come from a small fire a hundred yards off, but it was more likely to be a half-mile away. Even so, it was risky to get any closer. All four men quietly dismounted.

Brad was tired, but he was not sleepy.

"You rest," he told them. "I'll stand watch."

He wrapped his blanket about his shoulders and sat against a boulder, a huge rock that leaned over their small camp. The night was cool, but pleasant. He could smell the pungent, peculiar odor of sage, which grew in abundance in this part of New Mexico. But for him to smell it in this cool evening, someone very nearby had crushed it, perhaps a good bit of it.

They were not far away, and there were many of them.

Under the shelter of his blanket he lighted a cigarette, cupping its tiny red eye in his palm, liking the dry, hot taste of the tobacco. The horses cropped grass, a comforting sound. There was the smell of the horses, and the stale smell of his own unwashed clothing. That he would change when he got to Mexico. He would wear a clean shirt every day. He would bathe every day. This much he vowed to himself.

He drew deeply on the cigarette and snubbed it out on the ground. He got up and went among the horses, then he moved beyond the rocks, where he stood listening to the night, but he heard no sound.

IV

When it began to grow gray in the east, he shook Hondo awake. The big man got up silently, and Brad then stretched out and slept.

When he was awakened scarcely an hour later, Hondo was making coffee over a tiny, smokeless fire. Romney was saddling his horse. He could not see Jeffcoat. He had slipped away somewhere before daylight. Brad saddled his own horse, and then he saddled Jeffcoat's horse, then went to the fire for coffee.

Jeffcoat returned, coming in among the boulders and squating by the fire.

"Fourteen," he said. Indians. Mexicans. Anglos. An outlaw band."

Jeffcoat drew on a cigarette, and gulped coffee. "They are gone now, but they're following the girl and the old man."

"And we'd better be gone, too," Hondo said. "Will Kane can't be far behind."

Chapter 12

When it had gotten dark, Papa took up the lead rope and we started out from among the rocks.

We were mostly in the trees, but this was—after all—New Mexico, not the piney woods of East Texas. We got glimpses of the sky often enough, and it was not hard to continue our way south toward Santa Fe. It was possible, of course, that we were still being trailed in the dark—but unlikely. Anyone tracking us would not want to lose our trail. They would wait till morning. So every step we took bought us a bit more time, brought us a step closer to civilization and safety, and caused whoever was trailing us to wonder if we were worth the trouble.

I walked in front, then came Papa, leading the horse. Whenever possible, we walked over rocks or through thickets of fir trees, which were less likely to leave tracks if we were careful not to break off branches as we passed.

After a while we came to the opening of a canyon. We couldn't see it in the blackness so much as feel it. Cool air suddenly brushed past us. We turned up the canyon. It was a couple hundred yards wide at first, but in a mile or so it started to narrow and the canyon walls closed in around us. It was still night, and the darkness of the canyon was so deep we could barely see our hands in front of our faces.

It was wet in the canyon, and cool, and even though it was

summer and we were walking uphill, I nonetheless had a chill come over me that I could barely shake off. The only good news in that was it kept me from wanting to stop. Once, though, I did draw up short, and in the dark Papa ran into the back of me.

"Are you okay?" he whispered.

"Yes," I said. "You?"

"I'm fine."

And I kept walking.

I was tired, and more than a little scared, but I did not complain. I was a bit stubborn that way. I saw no value in complaining. If things were not going the way you wanted them to go, change them, or accept them. But don't complain about them. That's a waste of energy. I think I learned that from Papa, but Papa said my mother had been that way, too. Maybe that was what had attracted these two very different people to each other.

We walked about an hour up the canyon in the dark. Two miles? Three? I doubt that, but perhaps. It was nearly morning now, and altogether we had gone seven or eight miles.

"Used to be an ol' trapper's cabin up there." He gestured to the mountains ahead, and spoke in a whisper. "A cave, too. It was a hideout some of the boys used. There's a spring."

Something scurried in the darkness. The horse shifted his feet. Suddenly something bounded in the night, sticks cracked, the brush whispered. The horse jerked up its head at the sounds. Papa kept an iron grip on the lead rope, and after a minute the horse quieted.

"Lion," Papa said. "Probably smelled the horse." Then, after a beat, Papa added with something just short of a chuckle in his voice. "He may have smelled us, too."

As the night had cooled, the sky became crisper, brighter. The stars sparkled like diamonds against a jeweler's black cloth. The canyon narrowed and the walls closed in around us until—after another mile or so, the walls fell away and we were emerged into a shallow basin high on the side of the tallest mountains in the Pecos range. We found ourselves walking in knee-high grass, and I could smell water.

"We'll rest," Papa said. "Come daybreak, I'll get my bearings, and we'll press on."

I sat down, pulled my knees up to my chest, and rested my head on my knees. I was tired, exhausted. And I should have had other things on my mind—but all I could think of then was Brad. My world was so small then. When I allowed my little girl's imagination to run, it got no farther than him cutting wood for the fire while I fixed dinner. Or perhaps, if I allowed myself a real fantasy, perhaps I would go so far as to imagine him washing in a tin basin with his shirt off, his hair splashed with water and sparkling where the drops caught the sun.

And even these thoughts would cause me to flush with excitement.

Then I remembered he was an outlaw. Oh, he did not seem like an outlaw to me, even then when he was running for his life with $60,000 of other people's money. No, not even then. I've wondered many times since what that said about me. What it says about all of us—that we overlook what we want to overlook, though it is the plain and obvious truth. Our hearts play wicked games with us.

When I forced myself to admit that he was an outlaw, I wondered if he could change, as Papa had changed. Papa had changed when he married my mother. But when Mama died, whatever change she had brought over him did not seem to last. Papa did not talk much about it, at least not then, but it was his time with Father Dyer up in Colorado City that seemed to produce the real change. It sounded like a cliché to say he found God. Papa never described it that way, then or later. But something had happened. Something had changed. Papa had changed. I could see it with my own eyes, even if I couldn't explain it.

And whatever had happened up in Colorado City caused Papa to give up the outlaw life for good, and to seek out the daughter—me—that he had abandoned, and face the consequences of all that—including whatever resentment I might have had toward him.

Could such a change come over Brad? And what would it

look like while it was happening? Even then, even my 16-year-old self knew that it was much more likely that Brad would end up hanging from the end of a rope in front of some frontier town's courthouse than hanging sides of beef in a smokehouse we had built together. And the idea that his name would be on plaques hanging in skyscrapers he had helped to build—it was far beyond my imagining then. Indeed, at that moment, it seemed unlikely that I would ever even see him again—unless it was with his body propped up to be photographed, the way they often did with dead outlaws.

Did I know then that I loved him? I may have thought I did, but what does a 16-year-old girl know about love. I can say now: nothing. Or not much, anyway.

And yet…I wasn't wrong. Somehow, what I thought was love but wasn't at age 16 became love. How did that happen? Is it possible that we love not because of the lovability of our lover, but because we all want to see ourselves as lovers?

But these questions came much later. As I nodded off in knee-high grass in this meadow high in the Sangre de Cristo Mountains of New Mexico, all I knew, or thought I knew, was I loved Brad Bradshaw, and I wanted him to live, and I would wait for him to come to me from Mexico or prison or wherever God in his providence would have him go next.

II

Papa roused me from my dreamy half-sleep. "Let's get moving now," he said.

I scrambled to my feet. It was still dark, but the sky had brightened enough to kill all but the brightest stars. We were quickly on our way.

The climbing was steady now. In some places it was difficult even for the horse, and I found myself gasping for breath. How Papa made it I could not imagine, but he seemed made of raw-hide and steel wire. His movements were slow but strong and steady. At last we reached a cluster of rocks with a spring, partly shaded by aspen and fir trees. From the edge of the rocks we could see all around.

We had come out on top of the canyon, and it lay like a tremendous gash in the mountain, falling away steeply into its own darkness below.

"We might have done it," Papa said. He glanced at me. "But I got to sleep. Can you stay awake?"

I did not want to sleep. I wanted to stay awake and keep thinking, keep trying to put all the pieces together, not just of what had happened to me on this journey, but what was happening now, and what might happen next. If someone was chasing them, they seemed far away, even farther away than Brad.

"You rest," I said. "I'll keep watch."

Papa quickly fell asleep, and I had nothing to do but sit and watch and think.

I thought about what had brought me to this place. I had not been unhappy in school. In fact, school—especially literature perhaps more than mathematics—had been a way for me to forget I did not have a mother. As I told Papa, I could remember mother only barely. I had a few pictures, and it's hard for me to know for sure if I really remember her at all, or if I just remember the pictures I had of her. She was a slender woman. I remember her as tender and loving, but—again—I may be remembering what others have told me about her.

Papa had always seemed stern to me. I learned much later what a wise and gentle man he was—or at least that's the man he became. I also learned later that what I took for sternness was much more likely worry, or at least concern. He took his responsibilities seriously, and one of those responsibilities was me.

I also learned that a part of his sternness came from him not knowing what to do with me. Papa was a man who was sure of himself in most things. He handled horses and cattle with easy confidence. I could see that men respected him, some perhaps even feared him.

Up in Colorado City, where we had lived together for nearly a year, I had heard that respect from men like the banker, the sheriff, and even the big cattlemen around. It would be a cliché to say that he was "beholden to no man," but clichés don't get to be clichés because they are false. (That's one thing I never forgot decades later when we were making movies.) Clichés become clichés because they are true.

When men did not know I was listening, I had even heard them say to give Papa a wide berth, to stay out of his way. And, of course, I had seen what had happened with Romney and Hondo back at Rye Burns' place. Yet—and this became a marvelous thing to me when I got older—Papa became a good father and a kind man. He used to say it was because he had been forgiven much, and that made it easier for him to forgive.

But, I must also admit, in those days in New Mexico, he was still learning those lessons. We both were.

Papa slept now, curled up on the ground in the relative softness of a bed of ponderosa pine needles. Several times I got up from where I sat and looked around, careful to show no movement to any possible watcher below. Already I had acquired from Papa those habits of care and watchfulness so essential to wilderness life.

The sky grew pale, then red and gold, and then blue. The shadows fled, somewhere a bird sang, the song crystal clear in the morning air. The trees turned from gray to green, and the rocks all around from black to gray. Morning had arrived.

Papa still slept. Now, relaxed in the shade of a boulder, his face for the first time looked old, and for the first time I thought what this must mean to him, to be starting over again at his age, to be making a new life, for himself and for me.

There was strength in him still, that much had become obvious to me. Another of Papa's favorite sayings was, "I'm not as good as I once was, but once I'm as good as I ever was." He would laugh when he said that, or if he said it when others were around, it would be sure to draw a chuckle out of them. But he was right. Time had taken from him things that would never be returned, but it had also given him a sense of what he was able to do, a decisiveness, a resilience.

The sky was fully lit now, and when I looked around again I

saw a man sitting on a horse. He was not more than a hundred yards away, and he was looking straight at us.

III

Brad and his boys came along at a fast pace. They knew we were ahead, and they wanted to get to us as soon as possible. Brad could tell that our horse was limping badly and would be no use at all if we had to run for it.

Romney mopped his face and tried to ease his position in the saddle. Their eyes were constantly moving, searching, watching. They were carrying more money than they had ever had in their lives, or were likely to have again.

"Man," Romney said suddenly. "I'd like to have seen their faces back in Cimarron."

Nobody replied. Somehow, robbing the bank in Cimarron seemed a small thing today.

Romney stared at the others belligerently, but they ignored him. Well, nobody else had ever done it, had they? And they had. He could tell the girls down in Chihuahua that he was part of the gang that had stood up the bank in Cimarron. That would make them all sit up and listen.

Their eyes were reading the trail sign. An old man and a young girl were leading a crippled horse through wild country, and they had no way of knowing they were being stalked.

Suddenly a flock of quail burst from the brush some fifty yards ahead and to the left. It was more than enough warning. The four men broke off the trail instantly and vanished in different directions into the brush.

Brad had peeled off to the left. His horse had scrambled down into a dry wash that ran next to their trail. He slid quickly down off his horse, rifle in hand, and crawled back up to the lip of the wash, still facing south, the direction they were headed. From the lip of a dry wash, Brad held his Winchester steady while his eyes searched for a target. Hondo had gone into the same wash some fifteen yards up. The others broke right and were nowhere in sight.

For a minute, nothing happened. Brad glanced around at the wash behind him, saw nothing, and waited. He squinted his eyes and searched for whoever had made those quail flush. And then a rifle's sharp report ended the silence.

The shot came from somewhere up ahead, and it brought a dozen quick replies.

Less than a minute later, Romney came walking placidly down the wash toward Hondo and Brad. He was grinning.

"That Jeffcoat, he sees better than any man I know. I'll lay you five to one he notched one."

"Jeffcoat's not a dozen feet from where he was when those quail went up. He's got him a nest among the rocks on the other side of the trail."

Jeffcoat fired again, but nobody replied to his shot.

Brad mopped his forehead to keep the sweat out of his eyes. The earth felt hot, and the temperature here against the rocks was much hotter than it was when he was riding. His shirt was soaked with sweat.

Jeffcoat shot again, and a man reared up suddenly from the same wash Brad and Hondo and Romney were hunkered down in, but 50 yards up ahead. He threw his rifle out in front of him and toppled forward over a scrub oak bush, rolled off it sideways, and landed on the ground on his back.

Silence.

Suddenly there was a chorus of shrill yells and half a dozen men came from the sand and rushed Jeffcoat's hideout. All three men fired from the wash, and two attackers fell. Brad levered his rifle and fired again.

Jeffcoat had deliberately baited the gang into an attack to open them up for the guns of his friends. The marauders were tricked into thinking they had fled.

Minutes passed, long, slow minutes, and nothing happened. Then Jeffcoat came into sight, riding his horse. He drew up, looking around, and the three men came over the edge of the wash, leading their horses. Hondo was bleeding from a scratch on his face.

"Just a ricochet," he said.

It was their only injury. They surveyed the damage they had done. Three dead bodies. Two Indians and one Anglo. This was not cowboys vs. Indians. This was an outlaw gang—Anglos and Indians and probably a few Mexicans, too. It was hard to know how many, but based on what they had seen at Rye Burns', and all the shooting they had heard here, there had to be at least a half dozen still alive. With the kind of shooting they had faced from Brad and his men, they had beat a strategic retreat. But this would not be the end of it.

Jeffcoat spoke up. "They were here for the water," he said.

He pointed to a dry ledge in the creek bed—a ledge maybe three feet tall, a ledge that would have been a small waterfall in wetter weather. But even now there was water, if you knew how to find it. Jeffcoat rode over the ledge, swung down out of his saddle, and dropped to his knees in the sand. He started digging with his hands. Soon the sand was wet, and then there was water. They drank, then one by one they allowed their horses to drink as the water seeped into the hole.

A few clouds drifted by, but mostly the sky was blue.

"If Dave Stanton is smart, he'll get out of these mountains as quick as he can," Hondo said suddenly. "If he would head down out of the Pecos to the west he would hit the High Road between Santa Fe and Taos—and people."

"Stanton's smart," Brad said. "But he may not be able to. Not sure how we could have avoided the men we just ran into—even if we had wanted to."

"So you think they may be holed up somewhere?" Hondo said.

No one spoke right away, but they were all thinking the same thing. Papa and I had been steadily moving, but we were not going fast. Brad and everyone else could see that there was no way we could make it down to the High Road before getting caught.

"There's more than a few good spots to make a stand in these mountains, but they won't be able to hold out forever," Romney said. Then, after a second or two: "Do you think Will Kane's still coming?"

"I'm as sure of that as I am of gravity," Brad said, glancing at the trail they'd just come. "I can say without any fear of contradiction that he is what you might call…well, persistent."

"Does Kane know about the ice caves on the side of Santa Fe Baldy?"

"I doubt it," Brad said. "No, I'm sure he doesn't." Brad recalled the years he and Will rode together. "We never got this far south."

Hondo rolled a smoke, letting his huge body relax slowly. "Only the old ones know about the ice caves," he said. "But Stanton probably knows."

They squinted against the sun. Before them were the tracks of an old man and a young girl—and, almost wiping them out, the tracks of a gang getting larger by the hour as the worst of the worst were hearing from all around the countryside that $60,000 was making its way from Cimarron south to Mexico.

Hondo stared at the tracks, then blinked his eyes against the smart of the salt from the sweat trickling into his eyes.

Brad looked up at Santa Fe Baldy, towering ahead of them.

"Let's go, boys," he said.

Chapter 13

The man on horseback appeared before my eyes, spotted me, and disappeared so quickly and quietly that for a second I was not sure I had even seen him. But that second passed and I quickly shook Papa awake. By then, though, the rider had vanished.

"I think I saw something," I said.

"Oh, you saw it all right."

We had something of a view to the west, toward the Rio Grande Valley that separated the Sangre de Cristo Mountains we rode through from the hotter, drier desert mountains much farther to the west. We could not see those mountains, but in the morning light I could see the shadows of the Sangres recede across the near-desert to the west.

Papa had studied our situation in the vague light before he closed his eyes, and while we could be approached from all sides, there was a wide swath of low sage and dirt in front of us that would be essentially a free-fire zone. If they were particularly desperate they might try rushing us all at once, and if they did that, and there were enough of them, they might take us—but not before we would kill at least a few of them. So it was unlikely they would just rush us.

Besides, even to bad outlaws we were not worth dying for. Papa and I were in the wrong place at the wrong time, that much is beyond dispute. These outlaws were here not for us, but because they had heard about the Cimarron robbery and were hoping to get lucky, to come across the gang that had robbed the bank, and kill them for the money. We were just targets of opportunity, so to speak.

Still, I was a young girl, and they were not above...I didn't want to think about what they might do to me.

So I didn't. I just thought about what we would do if they closed in on us.

Papa placed me where I could do the best job of covering any attack from the obvious sides, and he took the other sides himself. The little circle of rocks we holed up in was small, and there was a little hollow sufficient to allow cover for the horse. The robbers would not be anxious to shoot our horse since it's possible that might be the only thing they got out of this encounter, so we held it close and waited.

"That Bradshaw," Papa began, taking up the conversation that we had left off hours earlier. After a pause he continued, "He might make you a good man. That is, if we all survive this mess."

I shot Papa a glance when he said that, but he kept his eyes outward. And I must confess that tears filled up my eyes at his words. In his own way, the only way he knew how then, he was giving me his blessing—no, not exactly that, but he was telling me that I could use my own judgment, and he was telling me that he saw in me what he had seen all those years ago in my mother.

Suddenly, with that one sentence, Papa had broken down whatever barrier there was between us. In my mind I could see the three of us together, Papa an old man, much older than on this day, and we were living in peace.

At this moment, it seemed a dream too foolish to indulge, and yet I did—even as I looked out over the rocks that provided us with meager protection, with a loaded rifle in my hand. I glanced over at Papa and saw something strangely alive in him. His eyes darted from place to place as he systematically scoured the ground in front of us. In truth, he was only in his forties, though in this country at this time few men lived to see fifty. And for all the wild living I was beginning to understand he had indulged, I was starting to see him as oddly puritanical. Yes, there was his new-found faith to account for that, though I knew little about it then. But also in the way he protected me, protected me even from Brad.

Not only that, though—and I don't think I realized this until this very minute—there was that light in his eyes as he stood guard over us. He was stepping up to his role as a father for the first time, to be the protector he had up until then never been. Is it possible that in that moment we were both facing death—or at least possible death—that he felt not fear or duty, but joy?

I do not know that I had these thoughts as I looked over and around the rocks that provided us protection from whatever might be out there, my eyes darting from place to place in that systematic way Papa had taught me, from clump of brush to clump of brush. Focusing on one place, then another—and imagining what I must do if they did come, and resolving that whatever I must do, I would do.

Still, I felt vaguely sick inside. I had seen cattle and pigs slaughtered, and I had killed game myself. But I had never shot at a man. It is a horrible thing to kill a man, to end all his dreams, all his possibilities. Even a bad man. Does he not have a mother or a daughter who thinks he might someday change his evil ways and follow the "straight and narrow"? When you kill such a man, you kill his dreams too.

So it gave me a sick feeling. Adding to the feeling was the idea that within a few minutes I might be dead myself, standing before God to answer for killing a man whose death extended my own life by only seconds.

That's when I saw something. I was making a sweep and was focused on a bush forty yards away, the last tall bush between the forest beyond and the bare ground between us. My eyes landed on a faint stirring on the ground, and I saw a booted foot slowly draw back.

I slowly pulled my rifle up to my shoulder and judged the

distance carefully. The bush was a dense piñon tree. There was no place he could get to quickly from where he had been, so I sighted into the bush a little to the left of where I had seen the foot, and a little above what I imagined would be waist-high for a man. If he was standing, this would be a gut shot. If he was squatting, then chest or head. I had fired a rifle hundreds of times. Thousands. That part, at least, I knew how to do. I took a deep breath, let out a little of it, then steadied the rifle on the target. The muzzle wavered a bit and I realized my hands were shaking. I squeezed myself even more tightly against the boulder to steady myself. Slowly, not jerking, I took the slack out of the trigger. Suddenly the rifle exploded in my hands.

The foot reappeared from behind the bush, along with part of a leg in blue jeans, but there was no other movement.

"I think I got one, Papa."

"Good girl."

Suddenly three men rose at once from the trees thirty or forty yards farther back and started toward me. I fired, but too quickly. All three disappeared into the brush, twenty feet closer.

Despite the commotion, Papa had not turned his head, knowing that it would be in that instant that they would be on the move. Suddenly they came out of the trees, running diagonally toward us. But Papa fired carefully. One man definitely went down. A second man dropped to the ground, but perhaps he was just diving for cover. Papa fired a third time into the bush he fell behind.

One more down. Possibly a third.

Papa wiped the sweat from his eyes. There was nothing in sight. Nothing anywhere. They were out there, but they were invisible. And they had lost two for sure. They must be doing the math now. How many men were they willing to lose for what was surely an uncertain prize? They knew we were not the Cimarron bank robbers, so whatever money we had was incidental. It had slowly dawned on me that I might be the prize they sought. And that realization had caused my blood to run cold.

Papa spoke: "Make every shot count. If we can hold them off

till nightfall, we can slip away."

But nightfall was a long time away. I glanced at the sun. It was still early. How long had we been watching out here? Papa shot suddenly at a suspicious movement of a bush forty yards away. But he hit nothing that we could see.

I was thirsty, and I had a bota bag filled with water at my feet, but I was afraid even to look down and grab it. I did not want my rifle out of my hands for even a few seconds. Our best chance was to pick them off while they were still too far away to make a bum's rush at us.

I glanced over at Papa. His eyes were red-rimmed from staring and from wiping them clear of dust. I had absolutely no doubt that Papa was prepared to die for me, and in that realization my heart filled up with love for him. But I also knew that his death might not be enough to save me.

"Papa," I said.

"Keep a sharp eye, Ali."

"I am, but I want to tell you something."

"What is it?" he said.

"If they rush us, would you save at least one bullet for me?"

Even before the words were out of my mouth Papa was talking: "Ali, don't talk like that. Don't even think like that."

"I will not let these men take me today," I said.

"Nor will I, daughter," Papa said. "That will not happen."

We both fell silent. Then, after a few seconds, Papa spoke.

"I love you, Ali."

Tears filled my eyes and I could not speak right away. But after a bit I managed to say: "I love you, too, Papa."

II

It was quiet as a morgue for another half hour. Then, suddenly there was movement all around us. I shot rapidly, twice, but I don't think I hit anyone. An Indian came out of the grass not thirty feet away, from a place I wouldn't have thought had enough cover for a rattlesnake to hide. Papa shot him through the chest before he was off the ground.

"Get one?" he asked.

"No."

Papa had grabbed a canteen and took a quick drink, slosh-ing the water around inside his mouth before he swallowed. He motioned for me to get a drink while he covered all quarters. I fought off the desire to drink and drink and drink, and put the canteen down after a couple of swallows.

Tension and fear always makes you especially thirsty, and of course there was the dryness and heat of New Mexico, too. So we had come by the thirst honestly.

After I drank, I looked around and assessed our situation. I was all right. They had been firing back of course, and a few bul-lets had hit nearby, but none too close to me. They were shooting on the run and would be lucky to hit us. Still, one of the bullets had glanced the boulder near Papa's head and a bit of rock had slivered off and cut his cheek.

And our horse was down. A bullet had got him, and he was kicking out his last breath.

It's strange, but on this day when I had killed a man, it was watching our horse die that caused my heart nearly to break. The man I shot was trying to kill us, so I honestly felt no guilt then nor any day since.

But the horse had done nothing but serve us, and watching his legs kick out for the last time—well, I don't know how to say it except to say that I think that's when the little girl died in me.

Papa could see I was upset.

"I'm sorry, Ali." Then, after a few seconds, "He was a good little pony."

III

All four men drew up sharply when they heard the shot—the far-off and ringing sound of a Winchester rifle.

Then more shots, a lull, and another shot.

Hondo spat into the dust, avoiding the others' eyes. "They're up high on Santa Fe Baldy. We used to call it Copper Park, for all the old copper mines around. I know that place."

Another shot, and then a ragged volley.

They sat their mounts, staring. Listening.

Romney had a look of resignation on his face. He took no satisfaction in this chase. He wanted to turn east out of these mountains and make the long race to the border. If Will Kane and the posse was still after them, it would end when they turned onto the high plains, for there was small chance of any pursuit catching up before they were safely across.

With sixty thousand dollars…in gold.

Brad looked up in the direction of the high mountains. His first thought was: ride toward the sound of the guns. His second thought: What got into a man that he would get his daughter into something like this?

But he knew. First of all, it wasn't supposed to be dangerous. By rights, this country had been tamed for years. Sure, it was plenty wild, with mountain lions and bears and snakes and in some places a long way from help.

But aside from a few outbursts like the Colfax County War that killed Reverend Tolby and a few others, this was peaceful country. No, Brad thought, I can't blame Stanton for wanting his daughter to see this country. Back east they talked about Colorado, and in California they held up Yosemite, but this was God's country, even Brad knew. Another thing Brad knew: If Papa and I were in any danger, it was in part Brad's fault. Brad and the $60,000 they were carrying were the magnets for all this trouble.

If the posse was still on their trail, any delay was dangerous. And Brad had no choice but to assume the posse was, indeed, still coming. They had probably brought extra horses. Trust Will Kane to think of that. The only thing they had going for them is that they probably had to stop last night just to be sure they would not lose the trail in the dark, and it's likely some of the men had turned back then. They would have seen the dead bodies at Rye Burns' place, and even though it would be obvious to Will and his posse that Brad had not committed those murders, they would nonetheless be a reminder that this was deadly serious business. The family men would remain behind on a burial detail, and they would go back to Cimarron after that.

In short, by the time the posse got there, Papa and I would be dead, or at least that's what Brad was thinking.

Hondo wasn't the only one who knew Copper Park. Brad had been there, too. It was a good place to defend, Brad knew—for a while anyway.

He fumbled with the piggin' strings that tied one of the bags of gold to his saddle. He tossed the sack to Jeffcoat.

"You boys have all the money now. I'm not asking you to come with me. I know it's a foolish thing. But I gotta do this. If I can, I'll find you in Mexico, and we'll split the money then." He swung his horse around. "You'd better high-tail it, boys."

He wheeled the big gray and spurred the horse up toward Copper Park.

Dust rose and settled. It drifted back from where he had gone, and settled slowly in the hot, heavy air. The other three men sat their saddles, watching Brad ride out of sight.

"It is a foolish thing," Hondo said. "But only if he goes in alone." Hondo turned up the trail toward Copper Park, too.

Jeffcoat wiped off the mechanism of his rifle and said nothing to anyone, but Jeffcoat never had much of anything to say. He was a square, solid young man, with a square, solid face and black eyes that were flat and steady. He let his horse walk four steps. Then he jumped his horse, not at the trail Brad and Hondo were taking, but up a draw that led onto a high shoulder of the mountain. It was a worse climb, but it would put him up above Copper Park, looking down on us.

Brad ran his horse for half a mile, then slowed to a trot. You could kill a horse running it in the heat like this, and he had a feeling he was going to need a good horse if he got out of here alive.

There was small chance of an ambush on this trail. For one thing, it was pretty clear that all their attention was focused on Papa and me. They would not be expecting an attack. Still, Brad carried his Winchester in his right hand, and after the initial burst, he rode carefully.

Ahead of him he heard the flat, hard report of a rifle, then several shots close together. Suddenly he went fast up that last hard climb and was racing his horse across the last draw before Copper Park.

Another shot sounded, and Brad wheeled his horse, standing in the stirrups. That was when I caught my first sight of him. It is impossible to say what I felt when I saw him standing in his stirrups, looking around to see where the gunshots were coming from.

I stood up, too. "Brad," I screamed. But Papa dove for me and pulled me back behind the circle of rocks.

A man who looked like a Mexican came from behind a tree near Brad and threw a rifle to his shoulder. Before Brad could get his own rifle up, a shot ripped through the Mexican and he fell face down onto the grass.

Startled, Brad looked around to see Jeffcoat sliding his horse down a steep gravel bank from the ridge above.

"Run for it," he yelled. "I'll cover for you."

Brad slammed the Winchester back in the scabbard and grabbed his six-shooter. He put spurs to his big gray horse and went across the flat in a wild run. Behind him, Jeffcoat was laying down a heavy fire from his Winchester.

He saw a man straight ahead of him lift a rifle to fire, and then the big gray was riding him down, the terrible hoofs tearing his body as they trampled him under foot. Brad fired and fired again. Men seemed to be appearing out of nowhere, rising up out of the grass in the meadow from behind boulders that were just outside the circle of rocks where Papa and I had been holed up.

I saw another man fall, and then the legs of Brad's big gray horse bunched under him as both horse and rider flew forward headfirst.

Brad kicked free of the stirrups and as the horse fell he left him, hit the ground, and rolled over. An Indian that had been hidden near where Brad fell started for him, but a bullet from

Papa's gun stopped him in mid-stride.

Brad knew they would have an eye on where he fell, so he lay stock still, flattened out in the grass. From somewhere overhead, we heard Jeffcoat still firing.

Suddenly the shooting stopped, but the echoes kept bouncing off the canyon walls for a few seconds until they faded away in the hot afternoon.

Brad told me later he could smell the crushed sage near him. The rich smell quickened his senses. He had ended up on his back, and he could see the sky, and without moving his head he could see a bit of what was going on around him, too.

He lay very still. Even I feared he might be dead, though I had followed every step of his horse's advance, and his flight off the horse. It did not appear to me that he had been hit. But there was no movement. Jeffcoat was no longer shooting. Had they gotten him, or had everyone just scrambled back for cover?

A bee, undisturbed by the fighting, buzzed near where Brad had fallen. My eyes landed on the bee, and that's when I saw movement. Brad was still on his back, the only thing moving were his hands. Without moving any unnecessary muscle, he expertly emptied the shells from his pistol and reloaded. Then he thrust a couple of shells into the magazine of the Winchester. The '73 would carry seventeen bullets, and he would need them.

He dearly wanted to lift his head and locate himself, get his exact position, but he dared not. In this deadly game the first to move was often the first to die, and he did not want to die.

IV

Hondo and Romney heard the shots, and they knew that Brad and possibly Jeffcoat had made it up to Copper Park. Their lagging behind was not cowardice, exactly, but it might also be too generous to call it strategy. It was true enough that they did not want this fight, but it would be unfair not to note that they were still riding toward the sound of the guns, not away from it, even if their advance was somewhat slower than Brad's. It is also fair to note that in the chaos Jeffcoat ended up with all three bags of gold, and it would not do for Brad and Jeffcoat to die and turn the money over to these bad outlaws.

So they would ride in, but carefully.

It's also worth noting that neither Romney nor Hondo could bear to leave Brad to fend for himself. They had ridden with Brad for several years now, and Brad had always been fair with them. More than fair. And you get to know a man when you sit around a campfire with him for weeks at a time, or fall asleep staring up at the same sky.

So it was a strange thing, this outlaw life. These men had thought nothing about robbing the bank in Cimarron—nothing except how to get away with it. But they were sacrificing their lives for each other.

Though not unless they had to. Plan A was not, of course, to die for your friends, but to make the other poor, dumb guy die for whatever he was willing to die for.

V

When the shooting died down, Jeffcoat retreated from the Copper Park meadow to where he left his horse, which had waited there obediently. He mounted and climbed a steep draw as far as his horse would take him, to a flat spot high above Copper Park where an old trapper's cabin stood, with its roof caved in. Jeffcoat hobbled his horse there, and he untied the three bags of gold and let them fall to the ground at the horse's feet, so even if the horse did get spooked and somehow limp away, he wouldn't take the gold with him. Jeffcoat then proceeded to the edge of the escarpment that looked down at the Copper Park meadow.

After a bit of crawling, slowly and patiently, he reached a place where he could see us, though I didn't know that then. I would occasionally look up behind us. The mountain towered overhead and was a virtual cliff to our backs, but it was conceivable that someone could have flanked us, so both Papa and I would turn and scan the escarpment above every few minutes.

I saw no one, not even Jeffcoat. But he was watching us.

He lay on his belly with his rifle in his hands and two pistols by his side, and all the ammunition he had been carrying. Including what was in the guns, he had 100 rounds, maybe more. There was still no sign of Hondo or Romney. From Jeffcoat's perch, he could see Brad, still as a corpse in the grass not twenty feet from our little circle of rocks. From there, Jeffcoat drew ever-widening circles with his eyes until he spotted two men who were closest to Brad, crouched behind a couple of scrub oak bushes in the middle of the meadow.

Jeffcoat sighted down the barrel, one eye closed, the other eye centering the muzzle on the closest man's spine. He was 100 yards away. He could hit a tin can—which was much smaller than a man's head—at this distance, but he could not afford to miss, and the Winchester's big .45-caliber bullets did not require a headshot to kill.

He sighted first at one man, then at the other. He did that a couple of times so his muscles knew how it felt to be trained first on one, and then quickly on the other. A fly buzzed near him, but he ignored it, not wanting to lose his bearings. He settled the stock against his shoulder, sighted the first man, and eased back on the trigger. The rifle wanted to leap in his hands, but Jeffcoat was already pushing the barrel to the left. The man below did not even scream, though the force of the bullet threw him to the ground with a thud. The other man was so startled that he stood up to run. That's when both Papa and I spotted him, and we both turned our guns toward him. But Jeffcoat had already fired a second time, and a bullet tore open the man's throat. He spun around and red blood sprayed all around as he too went down with a crash.

In that instant, Brad rose from the calf-high grass where he had fallen and came running toward me.

Chapter 14

All this time Brad had been hugging the ground, but he dug his boot heel into the dirt and the second he heard Jeffcoat's rifle he pushed out, and in one twisting leap he threw himself over a couple of smaller rocks just a bit nearer where Papa and I were protected in our circle of bigger rocks. Bullets snapped all around him. There were still more than a few bad guys out there. But Brad had made it that much closer to us, and now he was behind a few rocks himself.

Even so, he had to lay low and still. Jeffcoat would still occasionally fire from high above. He was methodically picking his targets and taking his shots. But the shots became fewer and farther between, as his targets undoubtedly wised up and stayed hidden.

I could look around the edge of the rock I was crouched behind and see Brad, though he had not yet spotted me. Only the smallest crack offered a view.

He needed just one more quick dash, and he was close enough to hear us without raising our voice. So Papa said, "Can you make one more jump?"

Brad seemed startled to hear Papa's voice. "You're here," he said. "You bet I can."

"Okay," Papa said, turning toward me. "Ali, grab your pistol."

I had laid the revolver down by my feet to use only as a last resort—if they got in close. Now I picked it up.

Papa continued. "There's a couple of men trying to flank us to the right. They're moving very slowly, but if they keep coming they'll get an angle on us."

I shot my gaze to the right, but I couldn't see anything. How did Papa know that?

"I'm going to shoot over there just ahead of them. That'll slow 'em down a bit. Let 'em know we see them," Papa said. "Ali, you shoot straight ahead with that pistol, but don't stand up. Just reach your hand around the rock and start firing when I tell you to."

I protested. "But, Papa, I can't see anything."

"It won't matter," he said. "We just want them to keep their heads down for a couple of seconds so Brad can jump through the crack here and into the rocks." Then, in a slightly louder voice: "Bradshaw, did you get that? Are you ready?"

"Whenever you are," came his voice.

"All right," Papa said. "Ali, let me get two shots off first. That will draw their attention. Then you start firing."

"Okay, Papa," I said as confidently as I could.

"On three. One. Two. THREE!"

Papa fired his Winchester, pulled the lever with a flick of his wrist, and fired again. I reached around the rock and fired at I knew not what. At that instant Brad rose up, took two steps and dove through the crack in the rocks just as a bullet whizzed past his head and shattered, sending lead and sharp rock fragments spraying all around.

Brad hit the ground next to me and rolled to get out of the line of sight of that crack in the rocks. When he rolled, he bowled me over. I stopped firing and landed on top of him.

Papa had stopped firing and ducked down, too, as soon as Brad was inside the rocks. It was all he could do to suppress a laugh when he saw Brad and me in a tangled mess in the dirt.

"Pull up a chair, son," Papa said with a bit of humor in his voice.

Brad and I scrambled back against the rocks. "I'll do that,

Dave."

No sooner had Brad gotten settled into a good firing position when we saw Hondo come tearing through the meadow in a full gallop. He charged his horse toward us and vaulted the rocks at the lowest place without slowing up a bit. Once inside the circle of rocks he threw himself to the ground and his horse barely managed to pull up short of the rock cliff behind us. There was an angry red gash alongside of his neck, and his sleeve was torn and bloody. Papa looked at him with affection and not a little bit of awe at what he had just seen.

"You never could stay out of a fight, could you?" Then, after a second: "Well, you're sure welcome here."

Hondo moved to the rocks. He carried an extra bandolier of cartridges with him. He found a place and settled down for a fight. And then out of a canyon came Romney.

They knew the horse, even though they could not see the man. The horse was running all out, nostrils spread wide, and Romney had flattened himself out as low as he could make himself, hugging the neck of the horse, Indian fashion.

Even as the horse seemed about to sweep past the hide-out, Romney let go and came sailing into the open space, one boot flying off by itself. He skidded to a halt, then looked down at a big hole in his sock. Bullets were flying all around, scaring his horse, who kept running through the meadow and into the woods out of sight. Romney surveyed his sock and grinned widely at me.

"You know any womenfolk who can darn socks."

I shot back: "I know one who can shoot, but none who can sew. You're on your own with that."

He turned and limped to the barrier before replying: "Well, come to think of it, I'll take a girl who can shoot over one who can sew right about now."

The odds had suddenly gotten much better for us. We now had five rifles in this circle of rocks, and one very clever sharp-shooter somewhere overhead. But we did not know how many were still out there.

"How many you think?" Hondo asked.

"Seems to me a dozen. Maybe more," Papa said. "And I'm guessing more on the way now that you boys and your money are here."

Papa did not mean the words to be accusatory, but what he said was true enough.

"Jeffcoat told me he saw smoke signals," Hondo said, "but I didn't believe him. Who uses smoke these days?"

"Some do," Brad said.

I looked at him. He was taking all this in. These rocks were not here by accident. Over the years they had been rolled into place for just such a moment as this, and we could hold out here for a while. But that would do us no good. The longer we waited, the more men would show up hoping for a share of the $60,000. Even a small share would be more than most of the outlaws and renegades and ne'er-do-wells who were racing toward us had ever seen.

And there was the posse, of course. We had no idea then if it was still coming, but Brad had to assume it was. He could not simply wait. But, then again, neither could the renegades attacking us. They had to know the posse was coming, too, and it's likely that half of those trying to kill us were also wanted men. So this business would come to a head soon enough. We quickly decided that it didn't make sense to shoot our way out. Our best chance was to wait for them to attack, or to make them attack if we could.

If I wasn't fighting for my life, I might have actually liked being up in this high basin at Copper Park. It was a lovely place, and for outlaws it had long been an almost perfect hideaway. There was water, there was grass, and without doubt there was game—though we didn't see any this day. In more peaceful times some wandering man who had reached the end of his wandering might stop and build a home here, and start a ranch. He would stay, rear children, sink roots deep within the sparse soil.

But that time was not now.

"Smoke," Papa said suddenly.

Their eyes followed his pointing finger, to where a tall column of smoke lifted easily into the sky, a smoke that broke, then broke again. A signal calling more men in for the kill.

We waited. I built a small fire and put on some coffee. It might have seemed a ridiculous thing to do, but they already knew we were here, and it was broad daylight.

None of the men stopped me when they realized what I was doing, though for a second they stared.

"I thought we might want some coffee," I said. "And there's a little meat."

Brad told me later that it was at this moment that he knew he would marry me, if I would have him.

II

High on the mountainside above us, Jeffcoat waited, too, but he was not just waiting. He continued to take pot-shots at any movement he saw below, and he would move after each shot. Jeffcoat quickly became our plan for getting the renegades to move. They couldn't simply wait to get picked off. They would have to try something.

And I would rather have him up on his perch than five more rifles in the rocks with us.

It was growing late. Already the afternoon sun was over the western hills. That sun was still hot and bright, and the air was very clear. But night would come, and Jeffcoat would wait.

Waiting was the first thing Jeffcoat had learned as a boy, growing up on the plains, and then on a reservation. Jeffcoat, like Brad and the others in his gang, had not set out to be an outlaw. He had engaged in petty theft to survive, and things progressed from there. He did not hate white men any more than other men, but he had become hard and bitter and disliked all men more or less equally. Brad, though, had treated him as an equal from the first days they met, and Jeffcoat had developed an affection for Brad that was about as close to love as Jeffcoat had ever experienced.

Some men love to fight, and they get good at what they love by long practice. But Hondo and Romney would sometimes say

Jeffcoat was a born fighter. It was bred into him. It was the manner of man he was. That was simply not true, or it was not more true of him than it was for any other man. It was a skill hard earned, reluctantly earned.

But he had, in some ways, grown to love it. Isn't that what Robert E. Lee said about war: "It is a good thing it is so horrible, else we would grow to love it?" Jeffcoat barely knew who Robert E. Lee was, but he would have likely agreed with him on this point. He was a boy in Oklahoma, living on a reservation, when the Civil War broke out. His parents were dead and he was being raised by aunts and uncles when he was being raised at all. Mostly he just fended for himself, slowly getting into more and more trouble until he fled to Colorado to stay out of prison for nearly killing a man in a fight.

Brad had taken him in, had become…not exactly a father, but a big brother.

Jeffcoat loved laying like this in the sparse grass. The sun was warm, the position good. But he knew at least some of the bandits below were looking for him. He could not stay here much longer.

From his pocket he took a dusty bit of jerked beef and, biting off a piece, he began to chew. From where he lay he was visible to nothing but the buzzards, and they were not interested in him…yet.

Jeffcoat watched the shadows crawl out from the cracks and the canyons, and watched the sunlight retreat up the mountainside and crown the ridges with golden spires and balustrades.

Coolness came to his lookout. He watched a signal smoke rise to call more outlaws to this growing conclave of bandits, but he merely chewed his beef and waited.

Fainter smoke came from the hide-out. That was a good sign. They were alive and hunkering down for a fight.

I never really knew Jeffcoat. Brad would tell me that all the stories Jeffcoat told—when he talked at all—were stories of war. To my knowledge there was only one story Jeffcoat ever told that wasn't about the war. It happened that just after Jeffcoat came to

Colorado he met a Mexican girl and they had "taken up" for a while on the edge of Old Colorado City. A group of soldiers rode up to their cabin one day and offered Jeffcoat money to guide them through the mountains. When he refused, they ordered him to. He was gone a week, but when he came back, the Mexican girl was dead, killed—they told him—by a grizzly bear she had accidentally cornered in a little box canyon near their cabin.

He had gone to the place where she had been killed and stood there for a while and smoked a cigarette, and then he got on his horse and rode away, not really knowing where he was going. One day, he told Brad, when he was cold and nearly starved, he killed a cow he found loose on the plains. He cut off a slice of the cow, built a fire and cooked it, and then a winter storm rolled in. He sliced the cow open and crawled inside and stayed there for three days and three nights until the storm passed.

Two cowhands found him. Jeffcoat didn't want to kill them, but he knew if they took him in he would be hanged for rustling. He tried to talk with the cowboys, but one of them went for his gun. Jeffcoat fired, not to kill him, but to keep the cowboy from killing him. Jeffcoat trained his gun on the other cowboy, who dropped his gun, froze in his tracks, raised his hands in the air. He made them wait—the first one still bleeding on the ground—while he cut more meat off the cow, packed up, and rode off.

They had come after him then, a whole posse of them, and he circled around and reached their ranch while they were gone and he butchered a cow by hanging it in the living room of the ranch house. He broiled a steak on their own fire. Then he took what supplies he needed—a new Winchester rifle and a hundred rounds of ammunition, as well as a couple of Navajo blankets.

Ten years later he met Brad, and he stayed with Brad because Brad, as I said, had treated him fairly—and because Brad was faster with a gun than he was, was a good tracker, and as good a horseman. Also, Brad was quiet, confident, and careful, and Jeffcoat understood those qualities.

Now he watched from above as the rocky basin turn from twilight into darkness. It was a beautiful place, if you could some-how lay aside the fact that we were fighting for our lives.

As he waited for darkness he located one by one the hiding places of the marauders. Some of them would bunch together now, but most of them would remain where they were, and that pleased him.

He noted carefully where each man had hidden himself. Then he waited for the first stars to appear before he got up and began his descent.

Chapter 15

Darkness brought a measure of peace to Copper Park. Somewhere an owl called, a lonely, haunting call.

Brad leaned against a rock and blew on the scalding coffee. It was too hot to drink, but he wanted it too badly to let it cool off. He sort of slurped it into his mouth, savoring each sip. We were all hungry.

Across the small circle Hondo and Papa lay side by side, sleeping on the hard ground, their rifles still in their hands.

Romney had found a high perch among the rocks where he could see all around, so far as the darkness permitted, but where he could not be reached by any prowling bandit trying to flank us.

I had let the fire go out as it got dark. But just before it became pitch black I had made a broth from jerked beef. I brought it and the coffee to a near boil before I let the fire die out altogether. It would stay hot—or at least warm—for several hours.

One moment—one second, really—is seared in my memory. A faint breeze came between the rocks and fanned the embers, and for a few seconds a blaze leaped up, lighting the little circle between the rocks. I turned my head and saw Brad watching me. Our eyes locked, and even though my first impulse was to look away, embarrassed, I did not. I stared into Brad's eyes until the flare disappeared as quickly as it had flamed up, and Brad's eyes disappeared into the darkness.

Up on the rock, Romney shifted his feet.

"Wonder what became of Jeffcoat?" he said.

Brad shifted his shoulders, trying to find a better place to lean on than the sharp rock pressed into his back.

Romney answered his own question.

"Mexico, I reckon."

"Not Jeffcoat," Brad said. "He wouldn't miss this for the world."

I did not know then just how true Brad's words were. When Brad had come across Jeffcoat up in Colorado City, Jeffcoat was a drunk and a candidate for suicide. It is not too much to say that Brad nursed him back to life, kept him off the bottle, gave him a reason to live. Granted, that reason was living an outlaw's life, but Jeffcoat had been so far gone that it was reason enough.

That's what a lot of people don't understand about being an outlaw. In a world that seemed to be spinning off its axis, which for these men it was, being an outlaw gave life a kind of meaning. It was a way to make a living, of course, but it was also—in a perverse way—a way for them to exert their own will over the injustices that drove them to be outlaws in the first place. I'm not trying to excuse the bad behavior of bad men. I'm just saying it is not completely irrational, or driven by hate. So while it was not a great reason, perhaps, to be a bandit, it was surely better—and by "better" I mean more meaningful—than the reasons that had turned Papa to drink or Jeffcoat to suicide.

So Jeffcoat now had a reason to live, and, no, he was no longer a suicide risk in the conventional sense, but there was nothing he would have liked more than to go out in a blaze of glory.

Romney made no comment. But I'm sure he was thinking of the money bags, which were all with Jeffcoat now. Sixty thousand, mostly in gold. He had never even seen that much money before, much less entertained the prospect of having a share of it.

After a moment he asked, "How many do you think are out there?"

"Dozen to twenty. Maybe more, come daybreak."

He looked around. We didn't think they would attack at night. A few of them were Apaches and they were famous for refusing to fight at night. Considered it dishonorable, or some such thing. But they weren't all Apache. In fact, probably only a few of them were Apache. And if they could see us, even faintly, in the glow of the fire, they might take potshots at us. So it was pitch black inside our little circle of rocks. Still, once our eyes adjusted to the night, we could see out. A canyon opened out of the basin to the southeast.

"Box Canyon," Brad said under his breath. "It eventually winds down to the Pecos River. We cross that and head down the eastern side of the Sandia Range, east of Albuquerque. It's a straight shot to Mexico."

The stew was still warm, so I passed a cupful to Brad.

"It's quiet," I said. "Are you saying we should try to escape in the night?"

"They're out there. We'd never make it. Oh, some of us might, but once they figured out what we were doing—and they would—they'd pick us off one-by-one."

I let that sink in before I asked, "Do you think we can hold them off?"

"Maybe. Till the posse gets here, anyway."

He let those words just hang in the air. The posse might save us, but it would mean they had caught his gang.

Or would it? Who knows where Jeffcoat was, and he had the money. There was nothing to tie Brad to the robbery. It seemed ridiculous, given the current desperate circumstances, but you have to remember that I was a young girl then.... I began to entertain the possibility that this might actually end well.

But all I said was: "I'm glad you're here."

"Well..."

He was for a few seconds at a loss for words, though he didn't have to say what I knew he was thinking: that he almost didn't come, and it was some sort of miracle that we were all here together and still alive. But all he finally said was: "I am, too."

We were sitting close together in the darkness. I was very

aware of the danger, and the, well, the ridiculousness of the situation. This was the 1880s. The West was won. Previously hostile Indian tribes were living on reservations. The railroads stretched from sea to shining sea. None of this should be happening. And yet here we were, holed up in an outlaw's hideout with yet more bandits trying to kill us and steal from us what we had stolen from others.

I caught myself as I thought that: "We"? "Us"? I had not stolen that money. Yet, how easy it was for me to slip into a place of hoping Brad and his boys made a clean get-away.

An owl's call quavered in the night. Then again.

"I'm surprised we didn't frighten away every owl within miles," I whispered.

"That was one of them."

"That owl? How can you tell?"

"I'm not quite sure, but I am sure. Something in the tone, I guess."

Suddenly there was a shrill, high-pitched scream, breaking off sharply.

"What was that?" I asked.

"A man died."

Papa came up beside us in the darkness.

There was no further sound. After a few minutes Brad said to Papa, just loud enough for Romney to hear too.

"Jeffcoat."

"That Injun y'all are riding with?" Papa asked, but before anyone could respond he answered his own question: "Could be." His eyes searched for Brad's in the darkness. "You think they got him?"

"No, he got one of them. Maybe more. Maybe only one of them had a chance to yell."

There was no further sound. The wind rose, and after a while Romney came down from his perch and woke Hondo. Papa took Brad's place, and the two younger men turned in.

I watched them roll up in their blankets, then I closed my eyes and drifted off, too.

II

When I opened my eyes, the sky had already started to turn from black to a dull gray. It was overcast, which was unusual for northern New Mexico as a general rule, though not during monsoon season. I sat up and tried to comb my fingers through my tangled hair. Brad was already awake. Papa was standing guard at a place where he could watch a wide area. Romney was still sleeping. Hondo was nowhere in sight.

The grass seemed gray. The trees were a wall of darkness. The brush was black. It was shivering cold.

Standing up, Brad slung his gun belt about his hips and picked up his Winchester. He checked his guns, one by one.

"Quiet?"

Papa nodded. "Yeah. Too quiet."

Just then I heard a low whistle and looked over the rocks into the darkness, but I could see Hondo. The big man had belly crawled out of our position and was twenty feet forward, tucked in behind the rocks Brad had dived behind yesterday evening.

Hondo motioned and Brad went forward, crouching low.

"What do you make of that?"

Hondo indicated an Indian, standing bolt upright and motionless on the edge of the brush. He seemed, at this distance, unnaturally tall. The Indian made no move. Brad stared hard, straining his eyes to see better.

"Hondo," he whispered. "That Indian's dead."

"Dead?"

"Look. He's tied to a tree, his feet are off the ground."

"Is it Jeffcoat?"

"It's not big enough to be Jeffcoat. No, it's one of them." Brad glanced at Hondo. "I'm guessing Jeffcoat's had a busy night."

They watched in silence. A gust of wind brushed the grass and bent it.

The wind made just enough noise to mask anyone crawling toward us in the grass. That made us all jumpy. Hondo lifted his rifle, but Brad touched his arm.

"Don't shoot at anything just yet," he said. "You might hit

Jeffcoat. He'll be using this wind to move."

Hondo waited, watching.

The wind gusted again and a gun flashed at the edge of the trees. Both Bradshaw and Hondo fired at the flash, and in that instant Jeffcoat broke, pouncing out of the grass and lunging for the rocks.

He collected himself in a crouch beside Hondo and Brad.

"Maybe thirty out there," Jeffcoat said. "I killed two."

Papa fired suddenly, quickly levered the Winchester and fired again. I found a spot where two large boulders leaned against each other, leaving a small opening on the ground. I wedged my rifle in the slot and fired at something moving toward me. It was still gray, and some of the attackers had painted themselves in black and gray and white. It was pure chaos for thirty seconds, a minute, perhaps more, but not much more. And they all seemed like moving shadows, ghosts. I couldn't tell who was Anglo, Mexican, or Indian, but I could see that my first shot centered on the chest of a large man. My powerful rifle stopped him in mid-stride, as if he had walked into a glass wall. The rifle he was holding flew out of his hand as he turned on the ball of his foot and fell down on his back and lay still.

I don't know how many had rushed us, or how many we killed, but as quickly as it started, the attack broke off. The attackers did not, however, run off. They dropped in the grass where they were.

The sound of firing ceased, and the air was still. The gray clouds hung low, hiding the morning. The dark red peaks of the mountains were touched by a shroud of mist or cloud. The grass bent before the wind.

Hondo fired suddenly, and we heard the ugly thud of a bullet striking flesh.

Brad shoved a cartridge into the magazine of his rifle. This time they would rush from a closer position. From my spot on the ground I thought I heard a faint, almost inaudible scratching sound. I scooted back a few inches and listened as carefully as I could, but I heard nothing more. Some small animal? The rocks almost completely surrounded me, and I liked the protection they provided, but I didn't like that I couldn't see all around, and I didn't like the idea of a chipmunk or worse nibbling on me, so I crawled all the way out and took up a spot where I was still fairly protected by the rocks, but could see all around, covering our left flank.

When they came again it was suddenly, and from all sides. I whipped my rifle to my shoulder and felt the slam of the recoil and the bellow in my ears. The smell of gunpowder drifted into my nostrils. I do not remember being afraid, at least not then. It seems strange to say this, but there was too much to do. I would sight on a man, squeeze the trigger, and lever the rifle quickly, trying to keep my eye on the target even as I brought the rifle up again. Often there was no target. I had hit my target and he had fallen. I did not think about what that meant then. I just found a new target, aimed, and fired. Aim, fire, lever. Aim and fire again.

A bullet whacked sharply against the boulder I was wedged against. I heard the ricochet, a ringing whine. Fragments of the rock splintered off and scratched my face. The attack broke and the sound that had been echoing in this mountain bowl rolled away. I paused to wipe my face and looked at my hand. It was covered with blood. I pulled a bandana out of my pocket and pressed it to my cheek.

I heard a coughing sound. Romney was down, choking on his own blood. Brad was beside him. I ran over to them.

When he saw me, he choked out a sentence or two: "You... you stick with Brad," he said. "He's the...best." He closed his eyes and gritted his teeth in pain. He tried to take a breath, but he mostly just made a wheezing, gurgling sound. Still he managed to say, "Hope you make it."

Brad put his hand on Romney's head almost like a preacher would lay hands on someone to bless them.

"I'm glad we've had this time together."

Romney smiled. "I guess I always knew it would end this way." Then: "Better a bullet than a rope." With that, Romney was gone.

A few spatters of rain fell. Brad went back to the rocks. We had lost Romney, but we had also taken a terrible toll on them. I don't know how many we killed, but it could not have been fewer than ten or twelve. Maybe more. So the bandits fell back. But they had their range now, and they were able to put bullets through the openings in the rocks out of which we had been shooting.

I could smell Brad's sweat and his unwashed clothing, and he needed a shave. That was one of the things I had marveled at when I first met him—had it just been a few days ago, north of Cimarron in the Valle Vidal? It was, and it had struck me then that even in the backcountry he had been clean-shaven. No matter what else was happening, he would find a creek and he always kept a bar of shaving soap, and he would find a few minutes each day to shave. But not on this day.

The shoulder of Brad's shirt was torn, and his shirt was wet with blood around the tear. Still, he faced out, and would fire at any stir in the grass or brush.

I did a quick inventory of what we had. Plenty of ammunition—for a while anyway. And if we could hold off till dark we could sneak out and grab the guns of some of the men we had killed. Water was a bit more serious. There was a spring at the edge of the cliff in this meadow, but we had to expose ourselves to get to it. Some of the coffee I had made yesterday was still in the pot. It was cold, but drinkable if we got desperate. Most of our canteens were empty. Only one full canteen and part of another. Not a lot for the five of us in this dry climate.

We faced west, with the cliff to our backs. But in the east the clouds must have broken a little, because we saw sunlight on the far-off peaks.

An hour of desultory firing passed. Nobody on our side was hurt, but every shot was a near miss. We didn't hit anything either, I don't think, or even see a good target. But we shot at anything that rustled or stirred. If they were sneaking up on us, we at least wanted them to do it slowly and carefully.

But that was not their next move. Just the opposite. They figured out that their attacks and retreats were doing nothing but allowing us to even the odds. So they came at us suddenly, more than a dozen of them. Some of them on horseback, charging at a dead run. We could hear their pounding hoofs as they built up speed in the trees beyond the meadow. When they burst into the open they were spread out and coming at full speed. We rose up to fire. They would be wildly inaccurate on horseback, and if we kept our heads we could pick off one or two each before they got to the rocks. But as we stood up to fire, the bandits that had slithered up or fallen wounded in the grass rose up and threw themselves at us, too. Their plan was to overwhelm us with numbers and speed.

I fired and saw a horse spill headlong, throwing his rider. Then a bloody Indian came over the rocks. Brad, gripping his rifle by the barrel and the action, ruined his face with a wicked butt stroke. He swung it back, fired at another, and was knocked sprawling by a bandit who came through a gap in the rocks. He lost his grip on his rifle, drew a .44, and shot the man in the face.

A bullet caught Hondo and the big man fell back against the rocks, gripping an Indian's throat in his huge hands. The warrior struggled wildly, desperately, but Hondo clung to his throat with crushing force.

How I remember all this, I'm not sure, because I was firing desperately, too. But I made each shot count. "Aim small, miss small," Papa had told me when I had learned to shoot. I did not aim at a man, I aimed at a button. If I missed the button, I still hit the man. And I tremble to say that in this sudden burst I killed three, maybe four, men. In a matter of seconds.

But just as suddenly as they rushed in, they retreated—at least those of them we had not killed.

I fell in a near-faint against the rocks. My hands were shaking. My whole body was shaking. I could see Hondo, on his knees, still gripping the dead Indian's throat. Hondo's shirt was drenched in blood, and his big ruddy face had gone an ashen gray. He started to speak, but could not. He died like that, on his knees with an Indian's throat in his hands.

Two gone. And the day was young.

Chapter 16

Not far away, under the same low, gray sky and a spattering of rain the posse, with Will Kane at the head of the column, pushed along the trail. They had not slacked off in their pursuit. The honor of Cimarron was at stake, and Will himself had been tricked by the fight in the corral.

Old Rod Taylor rode at the front with Will. Rod had been a cowboy in the Cimarron country for years, and before that he had guided the Army and others through these mountains, out of Ft. Union. There was no man in northern New Mexico you would rather have with you on the trail. He also had a fine singing voice, though that's a story for another day.

"Wherever they are," Rod said, "They're in trouble. I guess $60,000 attracts a lot of attention. I just can't figure Apaches being a part of this."

"Renegades," Will Kane said. "Mixed tribes. Mexicans. Anglos. Murdering thieves come in all colors."

Will Kane spoke with certainty, but he was worried. If Brad and his boys were holed up, the posse might be riding not into a standoff, but a pitched battle. The posse—which had 25 men when it left Cimarron—had thinned since then. Some had stayed back to bury the dead at Rye Burns' outpost. Others had families and farms to attend to, and Will had ordered them back. They still numbered a dozen or more—a strong force to bring in four bank robbers under ordinary circumstances, but the situation here had evolved into something that was far from ordinary. It was one thing to lead a posse chasing bank robbers who were trying to run away, but quite another if he got his friends killed by gold-lusting desperadoes.

He turned the situation over in his mind and reluctantly decided that if there were no results by high noon, they would return home. And it was not far from noon now.

He said as much to Rod Taylor.

"Maybe that's the best thing," Rod agreed. "But a man hates to give up."

Will Kane tried to recall everything he knew about Brad. It would be Brad he would have to outguess if the outlaws were to be caught and the money recovered.

Brad knew this country, that's for sure. When Will and Brad rode together as young men they had stayed mostly in the Cimarron country, but they knew every path, trail, and road between Cimarron and Taos, or Cimarron and Santa Fe. Will also had no doubt they were headed to Mexico. It was a long way, but it was a straight shot. It was a route that would reward determination and endurance, two qualities Will knew Brad had.

Taylor considered the matter and agreed with Kane.

"If we don't catch 'em soon, they'll be long gone. They're traveling light and once they hit the plains, they'll be traveling fast. And with all that money, they'll have no trouble buying or swapping for fresh horses along the way."

Then, after a moment: "What I wonder is why they hadn't quit these mountains by now?"

Lawrence "Boss" Sanchez was the best tracker in the Cimarron country. He had been riding ahead to check the trail, but he paused at the pass we had come by the evening before, the pass where the trail turned left, to the east, down toward Wagon Mound. Here was the answer to Rod's question.

"They didn't make the turn," he said. "They followed the man and the girl."

Will scowled and studied the tracks. At first they just seemed like a lot of hoofprints in the dirt, but Boss pointed and explained, and slowly the picture came into view.

"Are you sure that's the girl?" Will asked.

"Small tracks, light foot, quick step. It is a girl, all right."

"Awright," Will conceded. If Boss Sanchez said it was a girl, it was a girl.

Then Boss added, "First man and girl, and they've got only one horse. Sometimes they ride, sometimes they walk. Then many others—some Indians, but most not. Then Bradshaw and his men."

Rod Taylor eased himself in the saddle and bit off a corner of his plug of tobacco with a smile that was almost a snicker: "It amazes me how you got all that from this mess of tracks."

"Two people on one horse," Will Kane repeated. "They'd have no chance."

Boss Sanchez pointed at the ground and continued his story. "Bradshaw's men talk here. See, the horses move around. Want to go. Then one man goes off. The others follow, one at a time."

The members of the posse glanced at one another. All of them but one were western men, and they understood how Brad thought. Sure, he had made a big strike. He had sixty thousand in gold and a clear run to the border, but here was a man and a girl on one horse, in wild country with bandits on their trail, and they might not even know it.

The picture was plain. Bradshaw had gone to help, and the others had followed him.

"Well," Rod said, spitting a long, brown string of tobacco juice. "If that ain't a sorry deal. They're probably going to hang for helping an old man and a girl."

"There won't be no hanging yet," Will said as he turned his horse. "But this much is clear: the men we want and the loot they took have gone up to Copper Park, so let's ride."

He wheeled his horse and was off, and the others followed at a trot. But Will contemplated the situation uneasily. It was obvious that Brad and his band of outlaws had thrown over a chance for escape in order to help some people they could only have known casually, at best.

It would not be pleasant to arrest Brad after this, but they would have no choice. Arrest him, or shoot him.

Kane swore under his breath, and Taylor turned to look at him.

"Rod, he could have whipped me. He was whipping me. He let up on me—twice."

"Maybe."

"He was playing with me."

"Wouldn't say that," Rod commented dryly. "I saw that fight. There wasn't much layin' back, no matter what you may think. Bradshaw just needed time. He wasn't thinkin' of you. He was thinkin' of those boys at the bank."

Will Kane let out a low growl, as if he wanted to say something but couldn't form the words. He was angry with himself. All through the fight he had known something was amiss, because Brad was not acting like himself. He was never one to taunt a man—whip him, yes, but not taunt him. If a man was worth fighting, he was worth respect, and a taunt was disrespectful. Brad had been doing his best to get Will so mad he could not think clearly. And it had worked.

"Well," Rod said mildly, "at least it was one of our own. The Cimarron Bank was finally knocked over, but at least it wasn't any outsider who done it."

Knowing the humor—and pride—of the men who followed him, Will was aware that, angry as they were at being tricked, they were somewhat mollified by the fact that Bradshaw was one of their own boys. There were men here, men like Rod Taylor, who had punched cows beside Brad—and liked him. They did not relish the idea of arresting him, or shooting him, or seeing him dangle at the end of a rope, though every one of them would do their duty and—truth be told—the ones who were left, the ones who had not turned back, had a bit of nostalgia for those days.

Take Frankie Tolby. His daddy was a preacher who'd been killed for siding with the farmers in the Colfax County War.

184

Frankie was now mad at the world and never missed a posse. He pulled his horse up alongside Kane.

"Will, those Indians may beat us to it."

"You sound almost sad about that," Rod said.

"They're not Indians," Will said. "Well, not all Indians."

"Save us the trouble," Rod continued. "Though if they do beat us to them, it won't be a pretty sight. I don't wish that on Bradshaw, and I sure don't wish it on the girl."

Will touched a spur to his horse to step up the gait. The clouds were breaking now, and the sun was coming through. It was going to be another hot day, hot and muggy after the rain. Will could smell the damp earth, the way it smelled when the rain came after a long dry spell.

These men were family men, most of them. They should be at home, he was thinking, not out here in wild country chasing outlaws. How much was sixty thousand dollars, anyway? How many lives would it buy? How much sadness would it pay for if one of these men were killed?

Just then, somewhere in the distance, far up around Copper Park, they heard a shot.

The sound hung in the still air, and each man sat in his saddle a little straighter, but they did not look at each other. The shot was followed by the drum of rifle fire.

The thunder of far-off battle rolled down the canyon.

"What d'you think, Will?"

"Copper Park. They're making a stand up at Copper Park."

Suddenly silent, rifles ready, ears alert for the slightest sound, a dozen or so belted men from Cimarron spurred their horses and rode hard up the mountain.

II

Romney and Hondo…. Good men gone. No, not good men. Bad men, but good with a gun, and that was the kind of good we needed right about then.

Brad walked around the small circle and gathered their weapons, stripping each body of its cartridge belt and pistol.

Jeffcoat rolled a smoke. There was blood on his face from a scalp wound. I had tried to stop the bleeding, but he pulled his head back and gently pushed me away.

"I think we don't make it, hey?" Jeffcoat said, to no one in particular.

"Maybe," Brad said. "Maybe not."

"If you do and I don't," Jeffcoat said. "You take my horse." Brad shot his eyes in Jeffcoat's direction. "It's up there." The Indian pointed high overhead. "You know the Frenchman's cabin?"

Brad paused a beat, looking directly into Jeffcoat's eyes. Then: "I know the spot," Brad answered. It dawned on him what Jeffcoat was really saying to him. That's where he had hidden the gold. Brad repeated, "Yes, yes. I know the spot."

Papa levered a shell into the chamber of Hondo's rifle and stood it against a boulder. A loaded rifle ready at hand could be almost as good as an extra man. Not quite as good, but almost.

Jeffcoat turned to Papa and said, "If they get you boys, do you want me to kill the girl?"

The question was so matter-of-fact, so straightforward, that the shock of it did not immediately register.

A look of deep pain came to Papa's face. He knew exactly why Jeffcoat was asking the question, but he could not give the order to kill his own daughter. So I spoke up.

"Don't you worry about that," I said. "They'll have to kill me to stop me from shooting."

Brad and Jeffcoat smiled. Papa closed his eyes and turned away.

Jeffcoat drew on his cigarette. There was a swelling over one eye, and I wondered what had happened out there during the night.

"We make a good fight, though. Right? Many are dead," the Indian said.

We were making a good fight. It was no surprise. We were all experienced hands with guns—even me, though obviously not as experienced as Papa, or Brad and his gang. So it was no surprise that our aim was true. I had killed deer and even elk.

But I was finding out that killing men was a different matter. It wasn't so much the killing, as it was the seeing what you've done after the killing. In some ways it doesn't seem real. You pull a trigger and suddenly someone is dead. He's never going to breathe again. You take away all he's got and all he's ever going to have...all with the twitch of a finger.

But I tried not to think about that much—at least not then. I kept an eye on the meadow, and occasionally I would steal a glance at Brad. He looked down at the canyon. I knew he was thinking what I was thinking: Where was the posse? For me the posse was the only way we stayed alive, though I knew it would mean that Brad and Jeffcoat would go to prison—or worse.

The one thing we had going for us is that they likely didn't know how many of us were left. We had put up such a good fight, they would be reluctant to charge us again. On the other hand, these were dangerous, desperate men, and enough of them were so hot-headed and foolhardy that you could never say for sure what they might do next. And there were likely more—perhaps many more—on the way.

We all turned our eyes outward to the grass, the brush, the trees. Two men were dead, and neither of them had needed to be here. They had come partly from loyalty to Brad, partly—I knew this and it made me sad—because I was a young girl with a bright, fresh face who had smiled at them in a friendly manner, not knowing any better, not knowing yet the effect my smile had on a man. They were outlaws, yes, but secretly they were, to some degree, living the life of chivalry each admired in his heart. They were outlaws, yes, but they were outside a law they believed had been unfair to them. That didn't mean they didn't have a law of their own.

No sound, no movement. The waiting was the worst part, worse by far than the end of waiting. That's when I was the most scared, and the most sad. An occasional touch of wind rustled the grass and the leaves. The clouds were broken, the sun was bright on the mountains. Copper Park lay still under the late morning sun.

Suddenly a man showed himself, climbing to the high rocks that overlooked our position. If a few of them got up there, we would have no chance, none at all. The only reason the attackers had held off was that it was a dangerous climb.

Brad lifted his rifle. The man appeared out of the shelter of the treetops, climbing by hands and feet up the almost sheer face. Brad fired, and I saw his outstretched hand turn to a burst of crimson. The man started to slide back and Papa fired. The climber humped his back strangely, then fell clear.

And then they came with a rush.

Brad dropped his rifle and opened up with his six-gun. When I saw Brad do that, I did the same, shooting Hondo's Colt. I felt more than heard the roaring of his gun.

Out of the corner of my eye I could see that something was coming at me low and fast. Two men grabbed me and threw me to the ground. The face of one of the men was eye level with me. I could see the face through the gunsmoke. I could smell his foul breath. Then the metal barrel of a pistol pushed our faces apart as the barrel pushed his cheek and then his whole head away from me a few inches. Then the gun roared and the face disappeared in a red mist. I rolled away, and I could see Jeffcoat wrestling with the other man who had grabbed me. He thrust a knife in the man's stomach and twisted, then rolled off of him and grabbed his gun and started firing again.

Papa was fighting with a huge man, struggling for his knife. Brad turned swiftly and put the barrel of his pistol on the man's head and shot him through the temple. Papa's eyes turn toward Brad, in a silent thanks, but then Brad was down, fighting with a stocky man.

Brad struggled up, but the man he was fighting had bitten him in the side and was holding on by his teeth. I grabbed a gun laying nearby and shot a man coming over the rock barrier. Just then I saw Jeffcoat fall to his knees, though he continued to flay about with the same Bowie knife he had used to kill the man who had tackled me. At that instant, two or three bullets seemed to strike him at once. He was knocked clear around and fell back against the rocks, and as he caught my eye, he seemed about to smile.

Just then someone grabbed me from behind again. This time it was Brad who lunged in and hit my attacker in the head with the butt of his six-shooter. As he fell away, Brad shot into him.

The blast of his gun and the lunge at the man caused Brad to lose his grip on his pistol. He scrambled for the Bowie knife Jeffcoat had dropped, and threw himself between me and several others who were trying to grab me.

He slashed left and right, and his blade turned red. His shirt was torn from his body, and he fought like a man gone berserk, until the bandits fell back. Still in a frenzy, Brad rushed after them, out of the circle of rocks, searching right and left for an enemy to strike at. He realized then that in his frenzy he was completely exposed. I screamed at him, "Brad." Even before he spun around I had thrown him Hondo's loaded Winchester, the one I had leaned against the rocks.

He caught it in midair, and turned and continued to run after the attackers—still not entirely in his right mind after the desperate fight. But adrenaline or testosterone or anger or fear or whatever it is that fuels a man in such moments was fueling Brad, making his eyes wide and his mind a confused jumble of non-thoughts. He ran only a few steps, though, before he stumbled and fell face-down in wet grass. He tried to get up, but could only crawl forward. He felt the shadow of brush around him, and he crawled like an animal, deeper into the scrub. The last thing he could remember before he fell over a small rock escarpment—he told me later—was me screaming his name.

III

The Cimarron posse, led by Will Kane, came into the meadow with a rush. They came spread out in a ragged picket line, and they came with a thunder of hoofs.

Racing up, guns ready, they rode into Copper Park, but it was into a dead silence. The basin was empty. Smoke and the smell of gunpowder filled the air, but where there had been a storm of rifle and pistol fire just seconds earlier, there was now no sound but that of the soft wind. High overhead a buzzard circled, soon to be joined by another.

The posse slowed to a funeral pace. These men, though family men today, had not always been, and they had been on battle-fields before. They knew almost before they started seeing the bodies littered around our rock fortress that they were riding into a place of death.

A lone gray gelding stood by a clump of scrub oak—Brad's horse. On the ground, abandoned by the fleeing desperadoes, were the still forms of many dead men.

Will Kane rode up to the circle of rocks.

Papa stood up slowly. Will Kane told me many years later that he looked like something out of a ghost story. I quickly rushed to Papa's side, in part to hold him up, in part to feel him by my side. My shirt was badly torn. Indeed, it was barely hanging on me. I saw one or two of the men avert their eyes. I did my best to cover myself up.

"Well," Papa said, collecting himself as best he could. "You boys got here just in time."

Will Kane looked past him into the ring of rocks, then walked his horse still closer. From the saddle he could see into the rough circle that had been our defensive position.

He saw a dead Mexican, then Hondo, lying half under the rocks, cartridges spilled on the ground near him. The Indian he had throttled lay beside him in death.

Hondo…the big man was wanted in seven states. And Rom-ney…as tough and thin as a steel wire, dangerous, quick to shoot off his mouth and his gun. He lay where he had taken his last bullet. The gravel near his mouth was dark with blood.

"Where's the money?" Rod Taylor said.

But Will Kane and the rest of the men could not speak. A few of the men were old enough to have fought in the Civil War, and all of them had seen death before, but this was not like any of them had seen in a very long time, and—for some of them—ever.

I walked over to where Jeffcoat lay sprawled and dead. I took his huge brown hand in mine, and—for the first and last time—the tears poured out of me. I cried and cried. Papa came over and sat next to me and put his arms around me, but he did not try to stop me.

"Let it out," he said. "Just let it out. Cry all you want."

And we sat there a while until I had done just that.

While I was crying myself out, Will Kane's men surveyed the scene.

"It must have been one hell of a fight," Rod Taylor said. "There's seventeen or eighteen dead men out there. Probably more in the woods."

But Boss Sanchez had a concerned and cautious look in his eyes.

"We'd better get out of here, Will." His voice was casual, but there was no mistaking the urgency. "When they heard a dozen men coming from behind them, they backed off, but they'll be back, and there's more coming. That money's a powerful magnet."

Boss's words made only too much sense. Two of the men moved abruptly toward their horses, eager to get away. A third and a fourth followed. Most of the men had not dismounted.

But Will Kane was still not satisfied.

"I understand that," Will said. "But we didn't come all this way to go home empty-handed. I see no gold, and I see no Brad Bradshaw."

Will's words stopped everyone cold—everyone but Papa. He took a step toward Will and without a second's hesitation spoke out strongly: "Last I saw Bradshaw, he was bleeding in three places, and he ran off after the bandits like a mad man. I expect they shot him dead or he bled out somewhere down in those trees. If you want to walk down there and find his body, you'd better step lively, and mind you don't get yourself shot in the process."

"Besides," Papa added. "Didn't I hear it was three men who robbed the bank? Looks like you got your three dead robbers right there." Papa motioned over his shoulder at the bodies of Jeffcoat, Romney, and Hondo.

Papa's words had a logic that cut like a sharp knife. Will Kane met Papa's eyes with a hard stare, but he realized in an instant—we all realized—that no man standing in this meadow had the stomach or the heart to find Brad Bradshaw—dead or alive. Will lowered his eyes and—I swear I saw this with my own eyes—Will Kane smiled.

"Brad," he said to no one in particular, and to us all, "you beat me again." Then, after a beat, he turned toward the woods below the meadow into which Brad had disappeared: "Fair and square, too. Go in peace, my friend."

The matter was settled. All except for one thing.

"Would you boys mind helping us catch a couple of these bandit horses? Ali and me lost ours—one on the way up, and one in the fight, and we still got a long way to go."

Rod Taylor quickly cut around a couple of the horses grazing in the meadow and with a deft motion reached down and grabbed the reins of one horse, and then the other, and led them back to Papa and me. Several other men rounded up three horses and threw the bodies of Romney, Hondo, and Jeffcoat over them.

Will Kane said nothing. He just walked over to his horse, and he stepped up into the saddle.

"You and your daughter," he said, looking at Papa. "You come with us. We'll see you started on your way."

Papa took the reins from Rod and mounted one of the extra horses. I tried to mount, but my legs wouldn't pull me up on the first try. I leaned my head against the side of the horse. I had done all the crying I could, but I couldn't stop shaking. Papa jumped off his horse like a much younger man and rushed over. He spun me around and held me tight. I buried my face in my Papa's face and just shivered.

"I know, little girl," was all Papa could say.

The other men were now all mounted, and most of them looked away. When I composed myself, Papa helped me up on the horse, and I noticed then that a few of them had tears in their eyes.

I shot an embarrassed glance, a weak smile, at Will and said, "I'm okay. We can go."

And so we did. I was so weak that I held on to the saddle horn with both hands to keep from falling off the horse, and my mind was so weary and numb that it was all I could do to keep from falling asleep.

Still, I could hear some of the men talking.

"They done some shootin'," Boss Sanchez said.

Kane looked over at Rod Taylor. "You got some tobacco, Rod?"

Rod patted his pockets. "You know, Will," Rod said. "I don't. Must've lost mine...back there at Copper Park."

They rode away down the canyon. The steel gray sky that had threatened to let loose all morning finally did. The men broke out their slickers and put them on without even breaking stride, but I didn't care if I got soaked to the bone. It was plenty warm, and the rain washed the mud and the blood off of me and made me feel almost clean again.

IV

That same rain roused Brad Bradshaw to consciousness. He slowly raised himself up to a sitting position, his back to a small rock shelf he had fallen over in his headlong rush. He felt himself up and down. There was blood on his leg, and on his side, and a nasty gash over his eye. But he could walk, and he still had the rifle I had thrown him in those final frantic seconds of the fight.

He stood up, steadied himself, and made his way back to the circle of rocks. The posse had taken all the horses back save one: Brad's gray gelding.

The reins of the gelding were tied around the branches of a scrub oak. Brad walked over to retrieve his horse and noticed a small bag at his horse's feet. Rod Taylor's tobacco. Brad smiled.

Once more in the saddle, he took the trail Jeffcoat had used and rode up into the hills above Copper Park. Soon enough he came to the old trapper's cabin, and he found Jeffcoat's horse—and the three fat bags of gold. He balanced one of the bags on his horse, and threw the other two over Jeffcoat's horse. He fashioned a halter and lead out of rope he found in the trapper's cabin, and—riding the steel gray—he led Jeffcoat's horse uphill, and to the south.

Soon enough the rain stopped, the sun came out, and within an hour or two—aside from a few spots under the trees—it was dry and dusty again. When he got up high enough to see out, he spotted a small dark spot, and a trailing dust cloud—the posse, returning home with the bodies of three dead outlaws.

On the highest part of the trail he stopped and took in Santa Fe Baldy, even further off to the south. He was above timberline here and could see the trail he had taken to this high pass for a mile or more. He was alone. No one was following. If the bandits had come back to Copper Park to finish the job, all they had found were dead men and dead horses.

There would be no riding with the wind now, no mad dash for the safety of Mexico. To the world, he was a dead man. A dead man with sixty-thousand dollars in gold in his saddlebags. This was the second chance no man truly deserves and few men get. Broken and bloody and with the sun setting in an equally blood-red sky behind the Sangre de Cristo Mountains, Brad made a promise to himself: "By God," he said. "I will not waste this chance."

He moved his wounded leg, easing the pad he had made over the wound, and walked his horse down the eastern slopes of the mountain range. He was weak from loss of blood, and very tired, but he would not sleep. He would ride through the night, changing horses as he went.

For now, though, the steel gray horse walked steadily, though not toward Mexico, but toward Lamy Station, where he would meet up with an old man and a young girl who loved him, and together the three of them would take the train to California.

Epilogue To The Second Edition
By Ebert Denby

The story of Brad and Ali Bradshaw is now well-known to film buffs, though it took scholars and reporters and even curious family members to bring the final pieces of this tale together.

They came to California in the 1880s, with enough money to start buying up land in the mountains north of Los Angeles. Because they didn't want to draw attention to themselves, they started small. At first just a small ranch, but the ranch thrived. Quietly, carefully, they bought more land, making the purchases by augmenting the profits from their ranching with some of the sixty thousand dollars stolen from the Cimarron bank.

Sometime in the 1920s, Ali Bradshaw started writing the book you have in your hand.

It was no secret to Hollywood that Ali Bradshaw was a writer. Her behind-the-scenes work on scripts became Hollywood's worst kept secret throughout the 1920s and '30s. The first film ever shot in Hollywood, D.W. Griffith's *In Old California*, was shot near the Bradshaw ranch, and legend says Ali was on the set for the entire shoot (it took only a couple of days) and was fascinated by the process. As L.A. and the film industry grew, so did the Bradshaw fortune. The city needed land, and the Bradshaws had it. But Brad never sold an acre without buying two or more acres farther out, and as Los Angeles grew, the one acre became two became four became eight—until Brad Bradshaw was the largest landowner in southern California, and soon he was building homes and commercial buildings and eventually some of L.A.'s first skyscrapers.

All the while, Ali was whispering in Brad's ear about the movie industry. She would find talented filmmakers and structure deals fueled by Brad's money—Cimarron's money. As the country's appetite for movies grew through the early decades of the 20th century, these movies started contributing enormously to the family fortune. And—back to my point—if a script was not up to snuff, she would re-write it, or punch it up. It is not an exaggeration to call Ali Bradshaw Hollywood's first script doctor.

For all that, this is the only book Ali Bradshaw ever wrote, and she never wrote it for public consumption. She wrote it for her family. And there's good reason to believe that it is unfinished—in part because she worked on it until just days before she died, as the prologue indicated. The date on the prologue, January 1942, was just days before her death at age 81, barely a month after the surprise attack on Pearl Harbor that changed the world forever. The mention of war in the prologue was—many readers believe—the foreshadowing of a planned epilogue. But it seems likely that this story, told entirely in flashback, is missing the epilogue she ran out of time to write.

The fact that she may have considered it unfinished may also be why she never published it. That's not to say that people did not know about this story—at least part of it. The love story of Brad and Ali Bradshaw is also a part of Hollywood lore. After they settled in California, they took religious instruction in the Catholic Church. They started having children one after the other, eight in all, though one son died in the First World War. A daughter born with Down Syndrome died of heart failure, in the early 1930s, a common malady in that era—and even today—for those with Down Syndrome.

But the story you have in your hands—and this is another reason scholars think it unfinished—evolved over many years. It had its beginnings at family dinners. The children wanted to know how their parents met, and Ali told them the skeleton of this story, of the two of them meeting in the mountains of New Mexico.

"Not just any mountains," Ali—now devoutly religious—would say. "The Blood of Christ Mountains, the Sangre de Cristo Mountains." And, in the beginning, she left out the bank robbery and the subsequent killing. But over the years, the times changed and she did too. Also, her kids grew older and were—she felt—better prepared to handle the truth. After Brad died, in 1924, Ali apparently felt greater liberty to write freely about those early days in northern New Mexico.

The Bradshaw children were the ones who—after hearing her tell these stories for years—encouraged her to write the story down. She did, over the years augmenting the original skeleton of the story with the recollections of Brad and—eventually—even interviews and research. She even got back in touch with Will Kane. In fact, their correspondence, now housed at the University of Southern California Film School, is treasured by scholars but—for a variety of legal and other reasons—has so far not found a wider audience.

The financial and legal affairs of Brad and Ali Bradshaw were complicated. They were—by any reasonable standard—very wealthy people, and even though there was little if any acrimony among the children, the business affairs of the Bradshaws included interest not just in real estate, but also in movies, licensing, scripts, and projects under development. And, of course, World War II interrupted or at least delayed some of these proceedings.

One of Ali's lawyers was, for example, called up to military service even though he was in his forties, in part because of his expertise in intellectual property rights. The Nazis had pilfered billions of dollars in art, manuscripts, and other artifacts. The U.S. government decided it would be cheaper to draft a copyright lawyer than to hire one, so they drafted the best one they could find—the one who did the work for Ali Bradshaw.

But I digress. The bottom line is that Ali Bradshaw's memoir was not formally published until the 1980s, though dog-eared copies of it were in the files of many among the Hollywood elite, and it became fashionable to crib lines from Ali's memoir and insert them into scripts as "Easter eggs," special treats for those insiders who had read Ali's book. Dave Stanton's soliloquy about the Rocky Mountains, for example, is a pivotal scene in the independent movie *Jeremiah Johnson*. Ali's reflections about killing men made it into Clint Eastwood's *Unforgiven*. Ali's comment that her "aim is true" even made it into an Elvis Costello song. The list goes on.

Two final notes in closing: Will Kane escorted Dave and Ali Stanton out of the mountains and down to Springer station, east of Cimarron, where they did end up taking the train south to Lamy, just outside of Santa Fe. Brad was there waiting for them—by then showered, shaved, and wearing a new suit of clothes. They continued south on the train to El Paso and if Brad had any second thoughts about fleeing to Mexico, this would have been the moment to do so. He could see Mexico when he and Ali and Dave boarded the westbound train to California on the brand new Southern Pacific Railroad that had become the nation's second transcontinental route just the year before.

When they arrived in California, Brad and Ali married immediately. Because Brad was still recovering from the wounds he received in the fight at Copper Park, Dave Stanton bought the family's first homestead. So as not to draw attention to themselves, they bought just a couple hundred acres near the present-day town of Pasadena, and after a few years they added to their holdings by buying land farther west, a spread that eventually included much of Hollywood, the Hollywood Hills, and Laurel Canyon.

Dave Stanton never remarried. As Brad and Ali's family grew, he became a beloved grandfather to the growing Bradshaw clan, and he was instrumental in the management of the ranch for a decade or more. Eventually, though, he retired from ranching and became a self-taught man of letters and an active Presbyterian churchman, never quite able to convert to Catholicism as Brad and Ali had. Though Dave Stanton knew Ali was working on this book, and his recollections obviously informed parts of it, he rarely talked about the Colorado days with others. The only time you could get him to talk about those days was when he mentioned the circuit riding preacher, Father John Dyer, who he said was "the man who led me back to the Lord when I'd lost my way."

But when Colorado built its current state capitol, in the 1890s, the state solicited donations for stained glass windows depicting key figures in Colorado history. One of the stained glass windows is of John Dyer, unveiled in 1900. Officially, an anonymous benefactor made the tribute possible. Ali and Brad Bradshaw's papers, also now at the University of Southern California, makes it plain that Dave Stanton contributed the money for Father Dyer's stained glass window.

For all his close calls with death, and years of hard living, Dave Stanton enjoyed a long life. Born in Tennessee when that eastern state was still a frontier, he died in 1912 at the age of 89, with one of California's first telephones in the hall outside his bedroom, and a chauffeur-driven car in the garage below. He passed away in his sleep, with a copy of the Protestant reformer John Calvin's *Institutes of the Christian Religion* open on the bed next to him. His reading glasses were still propped on his nose when they found him the next morning.

Brad lived another dozen years, but by 1924 he too was gone. Ali, always an astute business person, presided over what was by then the family's significant affairs and vast holdings, making sure that children and grandchildren would never have to worry about money while also overseeing investments and writing large and usually anonymous checks to her church and other favorite charities—especially the Bible Institute of Los Angeles, which eventually became Biola University. After she began her correspondence with Will Kane, Kane would occasionally mention to Ali some need of the town of Cimarron—perhaps a fire truck for the volunteer fire department, or a church that was trying to build a new addition. Will would receive a check, with instructions to cash it and give the cash anonymously. The need would be met and the only thing the town knew was that "some old woman who had once passed through the Cimarron country and fell in love with it" had provided the money.

Closer to her Los Angeles home, she kept quietly writing and receiving supplicants—mostly screenwriters and directors asking for advice or money for their latest project.

When Ali Bradshaw finally died, more than 3,000 people attended the funeral. Only about 800 would fit into the church, so most gathered on the grounds and listened to the service on loudspeakers rigged up just for the event. A gentle rain—uncharacteristic for southern California—fell that day, but it did not reduce the crowd. Instead, umbrellas blossomed from the thousands gathered below massive steps to the church where the loudspeakers were stacked.

But at the edge of the crowd stood a man alone. He wore a cowboy hat, boots, and a khaki-colored rain slicker. He was old, well into his eighties, and after two days of travel he was bone tired.

Will Kane, by now long a widower and a legend among western lawmen, had outlived them all.

He had gotten the news within hours of Ali's death, via telegram. For reasons he would not have had to explain to Dave Stanton or Brad Bradshaw or Ali Stanton Bradshaw, Will rode his horse the twenty miles from Cimarron to the train station in Springer, even though he had a new truck, and there was a fine all-weather road between the two towns. The next morning, after a night in the finest room the Springer House hotel had to offer, he took the train to Albuquerque. The Albuquerque airport had opened the year before, and there was one flight a day to Los Angeles, with a stop in Phoenix.

Will Kane was on that flight, and the next day he stood on the edge of the crowd at Ali Stanton Bradshaw's funeral. Despite the rain, he stayed until the crowd disappeared, and he walked a block to the cemetery where Ali had been laid to rest next to her beloved Brad. Will reached into the pocket of his slicker and pulled out a handful of sage that had been growing wild by the Springer train station. He rubbed the leaves, now mostly dried, until they broke apart and once again gave out that strong aroma that carried him instantly back to the high meadows of the Sangre de Cristo Mountains. He tore the handful of sage in two and sprinkled half of it on Brad's grave, and half on Ali's.

"You beat us all, Brad," Will Kane said. "You, too, Ali."

Then he walked over to the busy Beverly Hills street at the edge of the cemetery, and he hailed a cab.

"Santa Monica," he told the driver.

"The Pier?" the cabbie asked.

"Can I see the ocean from there?"

The cab driver considered the question, and the obvious answer. Then he looked in his rearview mirror and saw something in the old cowboy's face that told him he'd better not crack wise, so the cabbie just said: "Absolutely. It's right on the beach."

"That's good, then," Will Kane said. "I have always wanted to see the Pacific Ocean."

Acknowledgements

I began the first draft of this book while spending the summer of 2014 in a cabin in Manitou Springs, Colorado, as the scholar-in-residence at Summit Ministries. Many thanks to the students and staff of Summit for providing the setting and the inspiration for this work.

Much of the action of this book takes place in and around the modern-day site of Philmont Scout Ranch, in northern New Mexico, where I served on staff in the 1970s and '80s. Early drafts of this book were read by Philmont's former Director of Museums, Steve Zimmer. His advice saved me from many embarrassments. It was Steve who, for example, told me that northern New Mexico was mostly sheep country until the railroads made it cattle country. This detail is just one of many I would have gotten wrong were it not for his expert help.

Jeff Segler, who I first met at Philmont more than forty years ago, has been a friend, road trip and hiking partner, confidant, business partner, and collaborator. I'm grateful to him for allowing me to use his beautiful painting "The Creak of Leather" on the front cover. Jeff also designed the front and back covers.

Steve Lewis of Eagle Trail Press is another former Philmont staffer whose publishing company is helping to preserve the history and culture of the American West. I'm honored to be one of the authors in his stable of fine writers.

Musician and cowboy historian Michael Martin Murphy read the manuscript, provided helpful feedback, and generously endorsed the book. I'm grateful for his encouragement and his friendship.

There were many other early readers of the manuscript, friends who responded to an appeal on the Philmont Staff Association Facebook page, as well as others who somehow heard about the effort. Those who offered encouragement and feedback include Joyce Baker, Heather George, Emily Hill, Bob Hostetter, Pam Howard, Don Huguley, Amy Latham, Stacey Locke, Robin Longinow, Charles Major, Abi McCoy, Bethel McGrew, Tom Munch, Ed Pease, Steven C. Rumage, Beth Shoemaker, Sarah Stonestreet, Michelle Ule, Heidi White, and Hanna Wilson.

A special thanks to my family: Missy, Brittany, Cole, Walker, and Morgan. All of them not only made my life interesting and meaningful during the writing process, but also read early drafts and offered encouragement.

Finally, careful readers of this book will quickly discover that it is an homage to the western novels of Louis L'Amour and Zane Grey, and to western and neo-western movies from *High Noon* and *Lonesome Dove* to *Unforgiven* and *Open Range*. Thanks to all the writers and directors who rode those high country trails before me.